Ida
~
Caught By Grace

By
Yolanda Magee

Ida, Caught by Grace
Copyright © 2000 Yolanda Magee
Published by: Horeb Publications
Cover design by Cathy A. Arnold

Publisher's Cataloging-in-Publication
(Provided by Quality Books, Inc.)

Magee, Yolanda.
  Ida caught by grace / by Yolanda Magee.--1st
ed.
  p. cm.
  LCCN: 00-134174
  ISBN: 0-9701988-0-9

  1. Faith--Fiction. 2. Spiritual healing--
Fiction. 3. Love--Religious aspects--Christianity
--Fiction. I. Title.

PS3563.A3445I33 2000   813.6
              QBI00-500065

♦ ♦ ♦ ♦ ♦ ♦ ♦ ♦ ♦ ♦ ♦
Dedication
♦ ♦ ♦ ♦ ♦

A Chance

A chance to be that is what Jesus offers me, with all of his riches and his glory, though men may smile and criticize, but none could they offer me, for upward I see the treasure that he has prepared for me and everyday I hope to lay one more block to my stairway to heaven

My house, my clothes and diamonds are fair, but they are not worthy of the jewels I shall find up there; the streets I walk now are paved with stones, but if only I await my heavenly home; A pasture out yonder somewhere I see; King Jesus with his arms stretched out to meet me

In Honor of Mrs. Ida Massey

♦♦♦♦♦♦♦♦♦♦♦
Contents
♦♦♦♦♦

◆ ◆ ◆ ◆ ◆ ◆ ◆ ◆ ◆ ◆ ◆
Acknowledgments
◆ ◆ ◆ ◆ ◆

Special thanks to my family for their encouragement and support as well as Christianna and Darian for their love and inspiration.

I would also like to thank the many men and women of God who encouraged me as well as delivered a word in due season.

Chapter One

CʒꙨꙨ

I Was Just A Child

Evansville, Kentucky is quite humid this time of year. It's July now and the blossoms are beginning to spring forth like never before. The ambience of it all is truly amazing. Here comes the mailman up the sidewalk with a package. It must be for me. I watch him closely as he fiddles around and then speaks.

"Hello!" Young lady, are you Ms. Ida Ford?" He asks.

I said yes, that is my name, as I rocked aimlessly back and forth. I signed for the package as he still looked at me.

He then said, "young lady, you look as though you have a story to tell." I replied, "I sure do."

"Have a seat," I said. I started out by telling him that my age hardly did me any justice. One could hardly imagine that someone so young had seen so much.

Hi! My name is Ida and one might say that I have had a hard life, but what do they know, they haven't been there everyday of my life. As I sit here in this old rocking chair and reflect back over my life it seems as though I've lived a lifetime in thirty something odd years.

It was a miracle that brought me to where I am today. It all started about three and a half years ago on a mild August day. Vileen and Stanley were driving home from a Wednesday night prayer meeting. They lost control of their car on the bridge.

The authorities tried to contact me but I was nowhere to be found. I was out getting high with my friends. By the time I got home the next day I was devastated to find out that they were both killed. It was even more heart wrenching to learn that Vileen had lived for about five hours after the accident. If only I had been there. There were so many things that I wanted to say to her but I just never got the chance.

I often wondered why God didn't take me instead. I was the one who was so disobedient and so rebellious. I was the one who had wanted to die for the longest time but instead he saw fit to let me live. Many nights after the accident I would cry myself to sleep asking God why he let me live.

"Why?" I would say.

After all I have refused to do for you.

"Why didn't you just take me instead?"

I never received an answer; I guess that I never really expected one either.

The fact still remained that Vileen was dead and there was nothing I could do that would ever bring her back. The funeral was on a Wednesday and it was sad, to say the least. I got dressed and headed for that old church that sat up on the hill. It was a special place for Vileen, we thought that it would be the most suitable place for the funeral.

We arrived there about 2:30 PM and it was the most sobering experience I think I have ever been through. After the preacher finished giving the eulogy, there came the moment of truth.

It was time for everyone to view the body. We all stood and row by row we walked around the casket. Then it was my turn and as I walked by the casket a million thoughts must have passed through my mind. When I reached the casket I took a moment to take one unforgettable last look at her.

I then began to think about how she had been so good to me. She always looked out for me and took care of me. And me, I was just too stubborn and now it was too late. Yet in that very same moment something hit me and all the tears and the pain just came rushing to the top. Somehow through that pain for the first time, I felt hope. It was then that I bent over and whispered in her ear.

I first told her that I loved her and then I vowed to her as well as myself that I would see her again someday. Not a single day passes that I do not remember the vow I made that day. It's what kept me sober, what kept me going sometimes when I felt like giving up.

I was glad that I could see my sister face to face just once more. It gave me so much strength. However, then I had to deal with a reality that I had never known. Vileen's death really hit me hard. I had to deal with not only her death, but I also had to face myself alone the best way that I knew how and there were no drugs around to save me.

Life was more than unbearable for me after the death of my sister. I was incarcerated for a year and a half for possession of drugs with intent to sell. My life was at rock bottom and there was nowhere for me to go.

Instead there I sat in that cruel cold hideous place, at times it felt as though I had reached into the innermost depths of hell and there was no way out. There were no windows, no doors, no freedom, no privileges for me, none at all. I had nothing but plenty of time on my hands, nothing to do but sit and think about my life. Vileen would often write me from time to time trying to reconcile our relationship.

I remember reading the letters that she sent me that last week. I read them repeatedly, and I could feel the reality in the words as they leaped across the page and I knew that she was correct about me, about my life once again.

One day I must have spent hours sitting, thinking about how Vileen always closed her letters. She would say that she loved me and that I was always in her prayers.

I know that it all sounds so simple now, but back then it meant so very much and I believe that it was from her heart. I only regret that I never told her, or showed her how much I loved her.

It hurts me to know that I will never have the chance to really know my sister. Her daughter Naomi, was the only thing that I had left here on this earth.

It was a glimmer of hope because I felt that perhaps I could someday have an opportunity to give and show her all the love I never shared with Vileen. Everything in prison was so sad. It seem as if I spent an eternity there waiting, hoping for some kind of breakthrough.

There were days when I stood there and peered out from between the white chiseled steel bars through the window from across the way. I was flabbergasted for the freedom that I might never again know. I feared that I would never have a chance to prove something not only to myself but also to my mother and my sister.

The mere thought pierced my heart and then some days when I would stand there I could see the reflection of the sun. It was shining so brightly till I knew I could just feel its rays beating down on my pale brown face. I missed so many things about the outside world. I had taken so many things for granted. I had no choice in when I was going to get up in the mornings, when I went to sleep at night and what I was going to eat.

There I was faced with the same old routine everyday. I knew that deep down inside a change had to come. I just didn't know how it was going to happen at least not yet I didn't. As the days began to pass I became sober and more sure of myself.

I began to gain a new respect and understanding of what independence meant. All of the hours that I spent in that tiny cell while looking back now I wonder how in the world I was able to keep my sanity.

I awoke each day having a routine that I would go through in my mind. I had a particular time for everything and that is what I believe helped me make it.

Then one day something did happen, a change did come. I had received a package and later the guard brought the package to me. I sat and wondered from whom it could be.

I was in shock, because I had no idea who might want to send me a package, yet it was lying there on my bed addressed to me. I sat there for a moment or two and peered at the package with amazement, as I pondered the contents thereof. I took a deep breath and opened the package; I was astounded at what I found.

Seven blue books were within the torn old shoe box. I picked up the first book and as I opened it the first line read;

"Memoirs of Vileen Ford, May 11, 1978."

The thing that caught my eye was that it was written in red ink. As I proceeded to read the first page I could see that this was going to be even harder than I had imagined.

I knew that by reading those diaries it would mean me having to open up all of those old wounds. I would have to deal with the fact that the relationship I would have liked to remember having with my sister was hardly the one that we shared.

Every time I would think that I had dealt with the issue, it would come up again. It became so easy to speak hollow words that had no meaning. The words flowed from my mouth so effortlessly because I knew that I would never have to confront her face to face again. So I just pretended that everything was all better between us although I would still feel that twinge again and then the denial. This forced me to confront another issue and that was that I had only been fooling myself.

All the tears, the pain, the heartache, and the lost years, what were they all for, I thought. Maybe I didn't have the assurance needed to deal with the real issues. Moreover, I knew that I would not only have to be strong enough to dig through the mire for the truth; but I would also have to be strong enough to accept it.

After I finished reading the first page I was really hesitant to read on because I wondered just how much did I really want to know about my sister. Was she really the sister that I always perceived her to be?

I guess you could say that curiosity really began to eat at me as I thought back to all the times that everyone just thought Vileen was so wonderful.

She was so perfect and she could do no wrong at least not in Mama's eyes, not in anybody's eyes. I always thought that she wasn't quite the saint that she pretended to be. I felt that maybe some small part of it all was an attempt to make me out to be the bad one.

There was so much competition between Vileen and me. I guess that is what drove a wedge between us, one that ultimately did mend but only too late. Many times we sought the unity that we felt we should have had as sisters but somehow we always managed to fail and so that day never came for Vileen. Sitting there I began to shake my head in disbelief. My poor sister was dead and there I was sitting, thinking such a thing about her.

There was still something deep inside of me that wanted to win the same thing that had driven me all of my life to the behavior that almost destroyed me. I turned the page and began to read. The first page of the book did not say much, just where we lived and how long we had lived there. Then the last line of the first page read;

––––––––––––

Hi! My name is Vileen Ford and this is my life.

More than ever I wondered if I was ready for this. I knew that those pages held more truth than I would care to know. I turned to the next page.

In big letters the first words that I saw read;

Memoirs of Vileen Ford, May 12, 1978

Today I was watching television in my favorite spot when my mother came into the den. She looked upset and she had been crying. She told me and my two younger siblings Ray and Ida to go to our room, the one room that the three of us shared. Since Mama didn't work a steady job and our biological father ran out on us right after Ray was born.

After we all got to the room, we heard a scream. It was Mama and one of her boyfriends fighting. It was awful. Soon I heard a door slam and about an hour later Mama called us to come and eat. We all sat down at the dinner table together Mama, Ray, Ida, and me.

We had what we always had some chicken, beans and potatoes. Everyone was quiet. It was plain to see that Mama had been hit. I wanted to say something and I wanted to help but I just didn't know how. After we finished eating, Mama picked up the dishes and placed them beside the sink.

She told us that we could watch some more television but then it was straight to bed. She never once tried to explain what had happened between her and her boyfriend Charles. She never said a word. She acted as if nothing had happened, but it did.

Then we finished watching another television show. We washed up and then we got ready for bed. Well, this ended another long and senseless day in my life but I only hope that tomorrow will bring a better day.

PS. Until tomorrow, better days ahead

The next entry in the diary read;

Dear Diary,

Today is May 13, 1978, and today didn't go much better than yesterday but I am still hoping for some way to make sense of this mess. This morning when I went to the breakfast table the first person I saw was Charles. Just as I figured, they had made up.

He politely gave us morning greetings as my siblings and I sat down to eat. I feel very uneasy because I don't like Charles much. I don't know why but something deep down inside tells me that he is up to no good.

Today was not like most other days for me. We got up first thing this morning and we went to the playground and played with the other kids. Sitting here thinking about today I did the silliest things. It is days like these that remind me that I am still just a child. It wasn't until lunch time that I decided to go home. When I walked in the door, I turned and asked Mama whose clothes were sitting in the doorway. She told me that they were Charles' and that he was moving in.

I thought I would almost die. How could she do this to me I thought? Why would she do this without asking me first? I just ran to my room and laid on the bed and cried because this was a man that I hardly even knew and how could Mama do this to me.

Later on this evening we went out to eat and had a great time. It was the most fun Ray, Ida and I had in months. By the time we got home everyone was exhausted. Mom put us kids in the bath and shortly after that Ray and Ida were fast asleep.

PS. This was one fine day

As I read through the next few pages Vileen said that everything went well for the next couple of months. I was startled as I read the next entry in her memoir dated October 20, 1978.

She opened by saying that yesterday was the worst day of her life. I could feel my heart as it sank to the floor. More than hesitant to read on, I paused for a brief moment but I then continued.

Dear Diary,

Today is October 20, 1978, and yesterday was the worst day of my life from the eyes of a child. When I came home from school, I found my mother lying in the center of the kitchen floor crying. I tried to ask her what was wrong but she only started yelling at me, telling me to go to my room.

I saw Charles sitting in his favorite chair and as I passed through the den I can remember him giving me this threatening look and yelling at me. I couldn't make out what he was saying because I was so scared and my heart was beating so fast.

I was glad to reach my room. When I got there, I saw Ray lying there. At first I thought he was asleep but then I quickly sensed that something was definitely wrong. Ida was sitting in a corner on the floor shaking.

I went over to my brother and I began to shake him; he did not awake. My heart begin to beat faster and faster. I was terrified and began to cry. Then I knew that I had to go get Mama no matter what. I ran to the kitchen as quickly as I could and I told her that Ray would not wake up.

Mom called the ambulance and soon after the police came. It was sure confusion around our house that night. Mama sent us down the street to one of the neighbor's house to spend the night. I knew right then that my life was going to change tremendously.

After reading the contents of the page I was nearly heartbroken because none of the events in the dairy I even vaguely remembered happening as a child. It was as though I was reading about someone else's life, and my heart ached for them as I read each word carefully. To know that this was a facet of my life really began to eat at me.

Many memories began to come to mind and none of them were quite so hideous as what I had read thus far. At first I outright denied that this was my life. But somehow in my heart I knew that if there was ever a righteous person on the face of this earth, my sister was the one.

As my heart begged me to stop, my mind edged me on for It knew that it would be best. I had to be able to come to some kind of peace with myself, I just had to.

So I put the book aside and as the days went by I would glance at it in passing as if it were some dubious task that ultimately awaited me. Then about two days later the desire became so strong until I knew that I had to finish what I had started.

I just had to, so one evening after lunch I picked the book up again and I resumed where I left off.

Two days later and we're finally home, I am really glad. The house looks the same except Ray is gone. That means Ida and I have more space in our room, but we all miss Ray. Mama seems to sleep a lot during the day and when she is awake she is very irritated and she seems very distant.

I hope she will get better soon. She is looking very bad, I think she might be sick. Today we didn't eat dinner. I guess she just forgot or she had so many things on her mind. At least that's what I keep telling myself. Last night seemed to last forever and dawn finally came seeping over that old building down the street.

I can remember watching the sunrise and set too many days to recall. I guess I find some kind of peace in it all, but for me peace ends all too soon because reality awaits. The next day finally comes and with it, such a madness that a child should never have to know.

Mama is drunk day in and day out. There is always a quest for the basics—food, shelter and clothing. This is no kind of life for Ida and me but most of all there is no love. I feel as if Mama has put us on a raft and pushed us out to sea and I can just feel myself drifting, drifting away. There is so much uncertainty about the future for myself as well as Ida.

But I think perhaps this is not the time to worry about the future. Instead I spend my days and my nights finding ways to cope with this new environment for myself as well as my sister.

PS. Until tomorrow, but I will never be the same

Chapter Two

⚮

Who Was She?

As I continued to read through my sister's memoirs I noticed that there was a huge break in the dates. Her last entry ended on October 20, 1978, and her new entry began March 20, 1980.

It only made me curious to find out just what happened between those years and just why there was nothing recorded in the diary, so I read on with much intent and intrigue. Her first entry was somewhat revealing but it still lacked the detail that I had come to expect from her. I have to admit that I did feel a twinge of disappointment but again I held it in as I read on through to the next page.

Dear Diary,

Today is March 20, 1980. Its been some time now since I have written you. I guess that it's mostly due to the fact that I misplaced you and I had no desire to look for you because the last couple of years I have fallen into a rut of not caring about anyone not even myself. I am ashamed to say that I am now on a path of destruction. I can see it but I wonder how I can stop it.

Things have been like this for the last year or so. School has become my mother, my father, my link to the outside world. I am eager to learn, there are so many questions that need to be answered about the world, about myself and so many things that my mind just can not comprehend.

I have to admit that I am more than a handful for those teachers at times. Why, I don't really know. I guess I just have so much anger and hurt bottled up inside until acting out has become a way of expressing my needs.

I've developed an inward yearning for attention and for acceptance. Neither ever seems to come. My teachers are all right I guess, they do what they are suppose to do but nothing more. There is no caring, no concern, but most of all no place for a little trouble maker like me. Nobody ever asks why Vileen acts the way she does; nobody really cares. Nobody but me.

Dear Diary,

Today is November 14, 1981. Its been about eight months now and I must say that I feel that I have wised up quiet a bit. I'm learning the system and I am doing what I'm suppose to do and everything looks better on the outside. Everything works for everyone else but on the inside I am dying of misery and shame.

At the age of fifteen I feel as though I have lived a lifetime already, there isn't much I don't think I know.

Nothing really matters much and mother hasn't really gotten any better over the years. I guess that she never recovered from Rays' death. Ida is doing well in school and she seems to have everything together. There are times when she needs someone to talk to and Mama isn't there for her. So I have become her sole support and companion.

Our bond has grown closer than that of most sisters. Yet in some twisted way I despise her because she takes what little love and attention there is from Mama and there is nothing left for me. But she is the only sister I have and nothing can ever change that.

At last this was my first glimpse at how Vileen really felt about me. As my eyes moved across the page sympathy began to fill my heart. I read about the relationship that my sister spoke of but it was so long ago that I honestly could not recall it. However, just to know that we once had such a closeness only made me want to know all the more what happened to change things.

As I glanced out across the hallway I could see the haze in the air. I knew that I didn't have many hours left before the lights went out. So I repositioned myself and began to read on with much vigor and intensity.

The next entry read;

Dear Diary,

Today is January 5, 1982. Junior high is really a blast, there are so many different personalities to interact with and for the most part I think I am doing well. Besides I am beginning to feel really good about myself. I'm beginning to understand a little about life and the outside world.

At first it was really hard to perceive that there is a whole big world out there and I am just another face among millions of faces.

But, "where is my place?"

"Where do I belong?"

I keep asking myself over and over again. After everything I have been through there has to be more to me, more to life, I think. Because everything in life happens for a reason.

PS. Until tomorrow, better days ahead

The next entry read;

Dear Diary,

Today is April 25, 1983. Today my best friend died and I must say that I am in a state of shock. I only found out today that Sheila had been ill for sometime but I never knew it. I couldn't understand why she would keep such a thing from me, I was her best friend. We were soul sisters, we did everything together.

If only I had known, maybe I could have been a better friend to her. Sheila was so proud; sympathy was the last thing she would have wanted. You would have never known that she had leukemia.

Sheila lived life as she always had. She should truly be an inspiration to us all. The lectures, the wisdom and love that she shared with me I want to share with someone else. As for me I am determined that her spirit will live on in my memory and that I will become the success that she always dreamed of being.

Sheila was one of my best friends, although she was about three years older than me. I was so inspired by her, everything that Sheila did I tried to do also. The way she wore her hair, the way she walked, the way she talked, I would have given anything to be like Sheila. She was the coolest.

Sheila was like a big sister to me, she looked out for me. She always asked me about my school work, asked me about my friends, she genuinely cared about me and I guess that is why she strove so hard to be a good role model for me.

Sitting here I can't help but think about her and some of the little sayings that she said from time to time. It seems as if she was always preaching to me about one thing or another.

She would say, "Vileen, find yourself a dream, something to believe in, set your mind on a goal and strive to achieve it." Don't let anything stand in your way, "because Vileen, she would call me, dreams are all we've really got." We can be stripped of our pride and stripped of our dignity, stripped of our money and our fame. But nobody, nobody can ever stop you from dreaming. "Vileen," she'd say, if you truly believe in your dreams then and only then can you make them happen. Sheila was a book of wisdom to me. She had lived a lifetime through her twenty something odd years here on this earth.

I feel sad at times and I think that maybe my sadness is merely a reflection of what Sheila was feeling down deep inside. She never was one to dwell on the negative things in life. She always had big dreams and I feel in my heart that she would have made it.

So here I am, my soul sister is gone leaving me with a gaping hole in my life. Now I am forced to focus on my own life, my own problems, and I would do almost anything to keep on pretending.

I really can't explain how I feel inside. It is as if a part of me has died and another part has been born. However, I am certain that it is a change for the best. The summer break is almost over and lately I've been doing a lot of thinking. A revolution has exploded in my life.

I've come to the conclusion that I am different now and that life for me will be different from now on. I don't want to be like Mama or Ida. I dislike who they are and the life that they have chosen for themselves. I know that in my heart I will always love them no matter what, but I never want to end up like them.

———————

Dear Diary,

Today is September 25, 1984. Last night as I lay in bed a thousand thoughts flashed my way. The one that weighed heaviest on my mind was the future.

"What does it hold for someone like me?"

All the odds are against me. I have every excuse for failure sitting right in front of me.

I am a poor black girl and I have an alcoholic for a mother. I don't have any kind of family structure. Yet somehow I still am determined that no matter how much the odds are against me, I must overcome them.

All I have ever known is what I have seen from day to day and I am sick of it, sick to my stomach. I love my neighborhood and the people in my neighborhood.

Mostly I am tired of the bondage that oppresses us, one generation after another doing no more than the one before. It makes me furious, and I am angry because I feel as if they don't even care about the condition of their lives. They seem to be content. However, I could be wrong.

Perhaps their contentment is merely hopelessness, maybe that is what I see written on their faces. It seems as if they have all but given up on any hopes or dreams. I must say that there are a few who still have a dream but that is all it is, just a dream.

I finished reading those last few words and the guards let us know that it was the third and final notice, that the lights were going to go out in about thirty seconds. I got up and scurried about trying to get myself situated before I was in the dark.

I just made it because right after I laid down the lights went out. It wasn't until then that I really had time to get still and think about what I had just read and it really troubled me.

I wanted to know more than ever what had I done to make my sister think of a friend as being more of a sister to her than I was.

"Why did she hate me so?"

"Why was she so disgusted with the neighborhood that we grew up in?" These questions plagued my mind as I wrestled sleeplessly. The next day came only too soon for me because in addition to coping with prison life I was also rediscovering my roots.

"Who was I then?"

"Who am I now?"

"Who was my sister and what happened between us?" Sometimes days would pass before I would pick up the diary again. It was the only way I knew to help me get through the pain just a bit at a time. It gave me the time I needed to absorb what I had read, analyze it and then digest it.

I would get so angry at Vileen sometimes and, oh, how I wanted to hate her but I just couldn't. After a couple of days the pain would pass and my anger would subside.

It was a couple of weeks later before I picked up the diary again but this time I started out bright and early in the morning. I could see the sun just breaking over the building across the street as I sat down on my tiny cot and got comfortable. I picked up the second book from the table beside the bed and took a deep breath as I began to read.

Book #2

Dear Diary,

Today is October 27, 1984. Yesterday I had the most intriguing experience I believe I have had in a very long time. I saw Retha walking to the mail box. She is a lady who stays down the street from us. No one in the neighborhood really cares for her because they say that she thinks she is better than everyone else. Because she graduated from some big university down in South Carolina.

Yesterday I decided that I was going to pay Retha a visit, which was a scary experience, one that will always be embedded in my mind. Retha is a tall, big boned intimidating looking woman. As I stepped up on her porch, she came storming out of the screen door.

"What are you doing here?"

I timidly replied, that I needed to talk to her and I began to tell her the stories I had heard about her and her unexplainable behavior. She then told me of her life as a young lady and how she graduated from school and landed a good job in Atlanta.

She said that she had big dreams about making things different for her and her family to be. As she continued talking I could see the hurt and the disappointment on her face. I could feel the emotions in her words. It was enough to make me cry. She said that her abuse of drugs is what tore her dream apart and by the time she woke up sober everything was gone.

The house, the car and the American dream, but that wasn't the most tragic part, she said. It was what she did afterwards that would impact her life in every way for years to come.

"What could be worse than losing everything you had worked for?" I asked.

She replied, that drugs were a bad thing that she allowed to happen to her. She said after she hit rock bottom she did absolutely nothing. "Can you believe that," she said. I just died spiritually and in a sense I still am dead.

"Vileen," she said, "people look at me today and they think that I am fine and healthy. I'm clean and I am sober. When I look in the mirror each day I don't see that. The image I see is one that is restless, troubled and dead. And so I gave up on that job, that house, that car and the American dream because I convinced myself into believing that I didn't rightfully deserve them."

"For many years I hung my head in self pity because the very life I had been running from I was forced to come back to. Everyone around me, my family, my friends constantly reminded me of the opportunity that I had for a better life and how I blew it."

She then said that with her alcohol addiction they didn't think she deserved another chance and by that time, neither did she.

So she just let the weeks, the months, the years go by and she did absolutely nothing. She just kept punishing herself over and over again for something she could not change.

"Vileen," she said.

"I know that it is too late for me, but, you still have a chance."

"Honey, find your way out of this hell hole. Whatever your dream is, follow it wherever it takes you. If you mess up along the way, then so what? Never mind what anyone else thinks. You do what you have to do because you are the one who has to look at yourself in the mirror."

Then I began to tell Retha about my plans for a new life and that perhaps they included me quitting school. She quickly corrected me and let me know that if I had any chance of making it out there, school would be the key.

I enjoyed my talk with Retha. She seemed to be a very intelligent person once you got to talking to her. So I decided that school would be a very important part of my plan. I am certain that Retha's words of inspiration will someday truly prove her divine wisdom. I am almost sure that my life is not the only one she has touched and is still impacting for the better.

―――――――

Dear Diary,

Today is May 12, 1985. I am going through a process of reeducating my mind, body and soul. I am trying harder than I have ever tried before. I'm doing my homework on time and doing well on my tests. I try to absorb everything there is to absorb. I am even taking a foreign language class and making new friends. I'm associating myself with positive things and positive people and disassociating myself with anything that makes me feel down.

I think I am well liked and well known at school and it makes me feel good. Although deep down inside I wish that every aspect of my life was the same way but thinking of home is difficult. Ida and Mama always make my heart ache. There is no talking to or reasoning with either one of them.

Mama is out there in the streets and Ida, well, I keep thinking that there may still be hope for her. Even though she has begun cutting classes, smoking, and worst of all, drinking. I want to believe that it is only because of the bad influences around her but somewhere in the back of my mind I know that, this is not the case.

―――――――

Once again I had to pause and wonder just what made Vileen feel the way she did. My perception of myself was hardly the one that she depicted in her diary.

As I read on I was beginning to get the feeling that Mama and I were just such a disgrace to her.

It only made me want to know why. I only hoped that somewhere within the pages to come I would find some answers to these questions. There was little time for me to analyze at that point because I could see from the clock on the wall that dinner time wasn't far off. So again I resumed reading.

The next entry read;

Dear Diary,

Today is September 15, 1985. CONGRATULATIONS, I've made it to my senior year and I more than anyone am most proud of my accomplishment. While I sit here today and write of the success I feel, I must say that it is also plagued with doubt about an uncertain future. Many nights I lie awake making plans for my entrance into the real world.

Although my plans include me getting a job, getting my own place and supporting myself. "The unanswered question remains how?"

"How I am going to accomplish all of these wonderful things with just a high school diploma?"

Yesterday when I got home I saw a car in our front yard. My first thought was that it might be a social worker, so as I got a little closer to the house I prepared myself for the worse. As I entered the front door I noticed a tall stocky woman standing in the kitchen.

"Hello," she said.

My name is Sarah and I'm your mothers' sister.

You can't imagine how surprised I was to find out after so many years that my mother had a sister.

This was a woman I never knew existed, then I turned to my mother and asked her why she never told us. But there was no reply, she was putting on some sort of air. Mama pretended things were a lot better than they were.

She told Sarah that she had a fancy secretary job that she was going to start next week. I've been saving up, she said and it would only be a matter of weeks before we would be moving into a new house on the east side of town.

It sounded good, too good to be true. Mama looked sober and sounded sober. I was happy for her. I really wanted to believe that perhaps this would be the new beginning I had always dreamed of. As night fell on our little house I lay in bed restless, struggling with the denial I had in my heart.

I wanted all the things that Mama was saying to be true, but would they? This is the question I asked myself over and over again. Later on that night I decided to get up for a glass of water and to use the bathroom. When I stepped into the hall I noticed that the bathroom light was already on.

As I tiptoed a little closer and peeped in, I saw Mama, she was having a drink. She didn't see me so I eased back down the hall and into my bed and began to cry. I was crushed, it was in that moment I knew that nothing was going to change, not now, not ever. Mama was an alcoholic and nobody could ever change that.

Nobody but her, only she had the power to do that. This morning when I went to breakfast, Sarah was there. Mama was still asleep; she probably had a hangover.

"Good morning, Vileen."

"Good morning."

"Are Ida and your Mother still asleep?"

"Yes," I replied.

"Vileen, how do you feel about your mother and her problem?"

"I don't know—I just don't know."

Sarah tried to explain to me what brought Mama to this point. She said, that Rays' death broke Mama's heart and that a few months after Ray died; my Mama's father died. Vileen, she said your Mama has never forgiven herself because in some strange way she feels responsible for both of them. This was my first time hearing about my mom's Dad so naturally I wanted to know more.

He was a good man but like everyone else he had made his share of mistakes in life. "Vileen," she said, your Mama blames herself for not being a part of her father's life. For a long time she would tell the rest of the family that she hated him. He had just abandoned her, but what else could he do. He was a restless man who had made his share of mistakes in life.

Then she said, "I know that deep down inside Paula (my sister) really loved her father no matter what the circumstances were."

Now it hurts me to know that Paula never got a chance to know Bobby or to let him know how she felt. She'll never be able to see him face to face again and to say all the things that her heart longs to say. All she can do now is to forgive herself for not forgiving him for all of those years.

"Vileen," she said.

This is the key to true happiness and self worth. Seek the simple things in life because there you will likely find the most contentment and gratification.

College is important and I wish that everyone could have an opportunity to go. However, she said everyone won't be a doctor, a lawyer, or a preacher. God gave us each a valuable gift and it is up to us to find it and use it—to empower not only our family and our neighborhood but everyone in the world.

Unfortunately, many of us never learn to assume the role that has been set aside especially for us, instead we choose to try to conform to the rules of an outdated society.

Sarah seemed to be a very intelligent woman and to me she represented a small percentage of women who did climb their way out of the ghetto and into mainstream American.

She inspired me very much and I began to look to her for answers in the short time that she was here. I was a confused young lady on the brink of a life-changing decision. I thought she was just the person who could help me get exactly where I wanted to go, but as always I underestimated myself and I over overestimated her.

The problem was she just did not want to get involved. She was a very proper person too so I shouldn't have been surprised to hear her refusal when I asked her to help me get into college. It was then more than ever I knew that my future and my pursuit of happiness depended solely on me.

I stopped and paused for a moment to put myself in Villen's shoes. Trying to understand what made her think the way she did. I had a feeling that I was just beginning to understand her. She felt as though it was her against the world. At times it seemed she had no one in her corner. Oh, how I wondered why she didn't come to me, but then I thought, would I have listened? It grieved me even to know that she was in such a position, and there was no one around to help. I read on as my heart continually ached for her.

Her next entry was on January 30, 1986, and she started out by saying:

"Where will I go?"

"What will I do?"

I am puzzled. Where would I start? I have so much fear. I don't know which I fear most, success or failure. The way I figure it, if I initially succeed then I will have to continue to maintain that level of success. If I fail then I will be forced to continue to try to succeed. The only other thing to do is to go ahead with my original plan. I will finish high school and then go on my way to achieve some life time accomplishment. There is still a part of me that does not want to take full responsibility for my actions, for my life. It would make things so much easier if there were someone else here to commandeer this huge endeavor.

That way if I fail there will be someone else to take the blame but there is no one else, no one but me. This is pretty hard to swallow for a 17 year old, although I feel very mature for my age and above all else I know that I am realistic. I understand that the path I have chosen is not an easy one but I know I have to make it out there. My senior year is almost over. The days seem to pass so very fast for me and the closer I get to the end of the school year the more frantic I become.

I have really screwed up this last semester of school. I got a D in English but what can anyone expect. I have too much on my mind and it's hard to focus.

Dear Diary,

Today is June 5, 1986. Yesterday was the big day. Graduation Day, finally arrived and I received my diploma. Looking back at last night as I walked down the aisle in my red and white gown and they called my name, Vileen Louise Ford. I was so moved by the feeling I felt. It is one I will never forget because I might not feel it again for a very long time to come.

I was determined that Mama was not going to ruin last night for me. She came to the ceremonies and after it was over she gave me a hug and a kiss. I was shocked! It had been a very long time since Mama had even hugged me, let alone kissed me. She told me that she was very proud of me and that she hoped my life would not turn out like hers.

Mama has the part of being the victim down to a science. According to her everything that happened in her life happened because somebody or something else did it to her—and me I am just the opposite. I have always tried to take responsibility for everything in my life as well as hers. But now the time has come for me to concentrate on me.

I had hoped that the feeling I felt last night would last forever. But this morning when I woke up the feeling was gone and I felt nothing absolutely nothing, I had no place to be, no school to go to. I felt lost as if I had just fallen into a river and I did not know how to swim but my feet kept kicking and my hands kept flopping, refusing to sink. Nevertheless I am determined to swim on my own.

This afternoon I took a walk down to the bus station. It has been a long time since I have been there. I believe I was about six years old the last time my Mom took us there. It was a lot different than I remembered. It's amazing how things manage to change so much over the years. I walked to the ticket counter.

A lady politely asked me, "where are you going?"

I just stood there with a confused look on my face because I did not know. Oddly enough it hadn't dawned on me. There I was standing in the middle of the bus station without a clue as to where I was going. All I knew was that I wanted out of this town and that was the only thing I was certain of at that point. As I turned and walked away from the counter, I began to ask myself over and over again where would I go. I knew that it would take some thought. After all this would be a very big factor in determining my ultimate success or my ultimate failure.

Chapter Three

CROSO

Where Would I Go?

Between the many pages that I had just read, I had begun to really examine my own life through my sister's eyes. I must say that at this point there was little I understood but still I knew that I must continue. Again I picked up where I left off.

Dear Diary,

Today is June 15, 1986. I don't know where to start. Yesterday I decided to go to the library. I thought that maybe I would have a brain storm. It had been a while since I had been to the library but I was sure that I would find something helpful there. I looked through all kinds of books on relocating, studying the population, the employment rate, and types of industry. I was still disappointed because I found nothing.

On my way out of the library a librarian stopped me at the door and asked me if I had found everything I was looking for.

I replied, "not really" and sighed.

Then she said, "what are you trying to find?"

"Information on schooling programs," I said.

She then began to tell me about a program that was available in Texas to help young people like me. It was a program that would train indigent young adults. They will help you plan a career path, she said. I was really grateful to her for helping me. Then she wrote down exactly where I could go and get more information as well.

I left there thinking that maybe this would be the break that I had been waiting for. Maybe this would be the vehicle to true independence and a building block toward a lifetime of happiness. When I got home I straightened up the house. Ida just happened to have her boyfriend over and they were in the front room fighting. But for the first time in a very long time I didn't say anything to them.

I just had entirely too much on my mind. When I got to my room I sat down and rested. I must have sat there for hours just thinking, just hoping that the days to come would bring more of an opportunity for me.

I tried hard to sleep last night but I couldn't no matter how hard I tried. I seemed to toss and turn all night long. When dawn finally did come; it put some of my anxiety to rest.

This morning I got up and got dressed and headed down to the bus stop to catch the bus downtown. As I stood there I began to think about how I wanted this program to be the answer to everything, I really did. Yet there was still a part of me that had to remain skeptical in case everything didn't work out. That way I wouldn't be so crushed.

The bus stopped and picked me up. Soon we were smack dab in the middle of town. I stepped off the bus, and I could see the Lincoln Building from where I was standing. I began to walk toward the old two story brick building and I was reminded of the history in that building. It was once a court house and years before that a slave shelter. As I got closer to the building my heart began to pound faster and faster.

When I got within ten feet of the door, I paused and took a deep breath as I thought to myself this is it. When I found the strength, I opened the door and walked inside. It was as if time stood still for that very moment. Everything felt so right. As I looked around I saw a woman sitting behind a desk directly to my left.

"Do you have an appointment?" She asked.

"No," I said.

"What is your name?" She asked.

"Vileen Ford." I replied.

"Thank you," she said as she wrote it down. "Please have a seat and someone will be with you shortly."

I was so nervous but after a few minutes a calmness came over me. I guess it must have been the atmosphere. The colors in the room were so lively and everything was so clean and neat; everything was in its place. A lovely flower arrangement graced the coffee table.   Everyone was quiet and everything was so peaceful.

I just wanted to sit there and enjoy the new serenity that I had found but just in that moment I heard a lady call my name, Vileen Ford. Everything ended, this was it. I got up and followed the lady down the long hall to her office. When we got there she informed me that her name was Ms. Bass and she began to tell me about the programs that they had available.

She then gave me some history that I found to be very interesting.   Ms. Bass said that Jobs for Young Adults was founded in 1969 by a well off couple in Texas. The program was a success there so it was duplicated through out the United States. She went on to say that the program was designed to help train young people who could not afford to go to college and to help kids who did not have a high school diploma obtain gainful employment.

I think the most important thing that Ms. Bass told me was that I qualified for the program. She then gave me a packet to take home and fill out.   I had three career paths to chose from Clerical, Technical or Medical.   The program was designed where I could go to school for twenty-four months.

I left there this afternoon knowing I had made a difference in my life. I felt confident and self assured that everything seemed to be falling into place. When I got back on that old bus, I just knew that I wasn't the same person. The ride home seemed as if it must have taken a lifetime, we would ride for a while and then all of a sudden we would come to a stop.

I can hardly say that I was there mentally because my mind just wandered and wandered. I sat there in a daze with this absurd look on my face. I can distinctly remember how quickly it all ended. This lady stepped on my toe in her high heeled shoes. What a rude awakening!

It was my bus stop and as I stepped off the bus it began to pour down raining. I took some of the literature Ms. Bass had given me to cover my head the best I could and I started on my way home. The sky looked dark and hazy, it was cold and the wind began to blow. I didn't have an umbrella, nor did I have a jacket because when I left the house this morning it appeared to be a clear sunshiny day. But by afternoon it must have been raining all over the world.

I know that I must have been a pitiful sight walking down the street. My hair, my clothes and my tennis shoes were all soaking wet. There was a sloshing sound coming from my shoes each time I took a step and water was running in my eyes, but still I kept marching determined not to stop until I got home.

Somewhere along the way I began to cry for no particular reason. Maybe it was because I was wet and cold, or maybe it was just because the rain depressed me. Still onward I continued to march until I had about two more blocks to go. The more I walked the worse I felt. I was overjoyed when I saw the house in sight.

After I got home the first thing I did was to get cleaned up; then I sat down to go through my literature. Most of it was still wet so I took the hair dryer and I finished blowing it dry. Some of the papers were spotted and bent up but it didn't matter to me because I knew that everything I ever needed was right there in front of me. As I sat there in the middle of the floor reading the brochures, I began to daydream about how things would be.

PS. Until tomorrow, still hoping for a brighter future

Dear Diary,

Today is June 16, 1986, and yet another day has come and gone. This morning when I awoke I felt awful my body ached all over. I guess sleeping on the floor last night had really gotten the best of me. After I went and cleaned myself up I started to look over the brochures once more.

The first one I looked at was one pertaining to the medical field. I thought that this would be great, being able to help sick people. However, on the other hand I was reminded of the time when this lady at the church fell down and scraped her leg really bad. There was so much blood, too much for me. So I quickly decided, that this probably was not the field for me.

The next brochure I looked at was the technical field. There were many different sub topics to chose from, but none of them were for me. At last I came upon the clerical brochure. This particular one I found most interesting. They offered data entry and computer programming as well as secretarial courses and upon completion I would receive a diploma.

I was really excited about this course of study. Now that I had selected a subject, the only thing I had to do was to fill out the pile of paperwork. I sat here all morning filling out paperwork.

I believe I must have finished about four o'clock this evening, too late for me to go downtown and turn my paperwork in, but now I had an enormous task a head of me. I had to find some way to tell Mama that I was leaving to go to school no matter what. So I decided to wait until tomorrow; that way I would have all night to get just the right words together.

PS. Until tomorrow, perhaps I'll put all of my fears to rest

Dear Diary,

Today is June 17, 1986. The rest of yesterday was a blur to me. Whatever I set out to do, my heart, my mind was not in it. It was as if the rest of the day had never existed.

Last night lying in bed I began to think of ways to tell Mama I was leaving home. I also want to be careful not to offend her or put her down for what she has or has not achieved in her lifetime.

But how can I get around the issue of her turning this situation around and blaming herself for my wanting to leave. Even worse, she might start blaming me for not wanting to stay. How will I handle this tomorrow? How will she handle this?

As these and many other questions rummaged through my mind, I began to feel the tears swelling in my eyes and my heart began to ache. I love my mother with all of my heart, but I also know that this was something I had to do. And for the first time in a long time I dreaded the dawning of a new day.

I knew that the day to come would ultimately mean that I would gain a long awaited ally in Mama or it would mean the loss of her as an important figure in my life. So today when I got up I made an extra effort to do everything I could just right. I rushed around the house to do all of my chores. I cleaned the windows, dusted and rearranged furniture.

Mama didn't get home until about two o'clock. She had been drinking. When she walked in the door, I asked her to sit down in the kitchen.

"Why?" She asked.

"I want talk to you."

"About what?" She asked in a stern voice.

I then told her that I had decided to go away to school and that this was something that meant a lot to me. I hoped that she would somehow try to put herself in my shoes.

I reminded her how she'd preached to us over and over again through the years about being smart enough to make better choices in life. After saying everything I wanted to say I was breathless; I had been talking a mile a minute. Because I wanted to get everything out before Mama had a chance to say anything.

When I looked up at Mama tears were streaming down her face. I didn't know what else to say so I said nothing. When Mama finally did speak, the first thing she said was, "Vileen, you must know that I love you." She then said, you are my oldest daughter and I would have given anything to be like you.

One of the things I admire most about you is your inner strength, your ability to seek after something until you've conquered it. It was really strange to hear this from Mama because she hardly ever spoke to me. She hardly ever spoke to anyone.

Mama said that when she was a lot younger she always wanted to go to nursing school but her mother never let her go because she said that it was too far away.

"I still regret not going," she said. Because staying here in Kentucky was one of the worst choices I believe I have ever made.

I understand what you have to do and if you feel that Kentucky is not the place where you need to start then I am behind you one-hundred percent.

"Vi," she said.

"Most of the time decisions are irreversible; that is why you must give careful consideration to whatever you are planning to do." She then told me that we may not always like the choices that we have made if we look back at some later date but we have to do the best we can at the time with whatever resources are available to us.

Mama then grabbed me and gave me this overwhelming hug as tears ran down her face. We just stood there entwined in this lasting embrace. I'll never forget the words she whispered in my ear, over and over again, she said "I wish you strength, Vileen, I just wish you strength."

Today Mama told me all I wanted to know. She gave me the approval that I thought I never needed from her, but more than that she gave me her love. As I left the kitchen, I could hardly move because emotions overwhelmed my body and I did not want the moment to end because the warmth in the air was long overdue.

When I got to my bedroom, I sat down and cried. I knew that my plans would have to be carried out because this would be best for me in the long run. I also wanted to show my baby sister that she too could do something with her life and to prove to her that it was not too late for her, that it is never too late.

Today was a very emotional one for Mama and me that is why I cherish it all the more because I feel that such a moment might not ever come again.

> *PS. Until tomorrow, then I will say my good-byes*

Dear Diary,

Today is June 19, 1986. Today I took the bus back downtown to the old Lincoln Building and saw Ms. Bass. I turned in the paperwork I had finished and she told me that she was pretty positive I would get the grant. I was elated.

There were three different states that had openings in their clerical programs. She said that I could go to Indiana, Texas or California. It didn't take me long to decide; I chose Texas. She said school would start in about seven weeks.

On the way home all I thought about was Ida. How would I tell Ida? Before I could finish one complete thought, another one would come, Ida was all over my mind. I knew that I had to talk to her and I knew that it was not going to be an easy task. Ida was all but the typical teenager. She knew everything. Literally there wasn't anything that she thought she did not know.

I finally arrived home and about two hours later, Ida came home with her boyfriend shortly there after. They were in the front room watching television. I could already sense that Ida was in a irritable mood but regardless I knew that I had to talk to her that night. Finally, Don, at least that is what I think his name was, he went home.

I carefully and quietly edged my way to the front room where Ida was sitting in the center of the floor. She asked what I wanted in her usual snappy voice, and I replied, "Ida, I did not come up here to fight with you."

"I came up here to talk to you." I began to tell her how I knew that we didn't always see things eye to eye in the past but the time had come for us to put our differences aside.

"Ida," I said. I'm leaving and I probably wouldn't be back for a while. I figured her response would be that she did not care and so it was. I was hurt, however I tried hard not to let her see because to me it meant giving in to her and I was not about to do that.

I made sure that I let her know that she was my sister and that no matter what I would always love her even if she didn't return that same love for me. I must admit that after my conversation with Ida I was pretty shaken up because Ida has always resented me. Why? I do not know, maybe it is because I am always the little miss goody two shoes. I am always the one who gets better grades, makes better choices, and Mama depends on me.

Looking back now I can honestly say that yes my baby sister has had a pretty rough life. She has the world to measure up to and she only knows what she has seen from day to day. But I guess I am fortunate to have a sister to love. After I finished talking to my sister, I laid on the sofa and I fell asleep.

PS. Well, this put an end to one dreaded day in my life

———————

Dear Diary,

Today is August 12, 1986. Now that the big day has come and gone, I decided to tell you about it. I woke up that morning with so much anticipation, more than one mortal soul should know, but yet at the same time I knew that somehow I must find a way to contain it.

I was determined that nothing was going to ruin my day. I was going to leave there in the right frame of mind. My mother got a friend of hers to take us to the bus station. The ride in the car was very quiet. I could almost hear a pin drop. I could feel the emotions in the air but no one said a word.

Then Mama's friend tried to make small conversation but a laser could not cut through the tension in that car. Finally we arrived at the bus station, the car stopped, and everyone just sat in the car. I did not want to be the first one out because I didn't want to seem like I was in such a rush to get away from home.

Finally, I opened my car door, we walked toward the bus station, and it became evident that Mama was an emotional wreck. I guess if she hadn't lost so many people that were close to her, she would not have felt as if she was losing me also.

After we got inside the bus station it just so happened that it was a very busy day. People were everywhere. I had to stand in a long line just to pick up my ticket at the ticket counter.

At last I reached the front of the line and I gave the lady my name. She then handed me the ticket Ms. Bass had arranged for in advance; it made things so much easier. Ida, Mama and I went to sit down and wait for bus number 251 to come. The bus was due in at about 2:30 PM and we were scheduled to pull out about 3:00 PM. I was so excited but I couldn't dare show it. I was bound for Texas and I just hoped that Texas was all that I had dreamed it would be. After all Texas could have been anywhere to me. It didn't matter, it was a beginning.

As I sat there I looked to my left and I looked to my right. Mama and Ida were sitting there with the longest faces I believe I had ever seen in my life. There wasn't a single word spoken between us. Once again Mama's friend tried to break the silence by making conversation with me about my plans once I got to Texas.

Mama quickly let Mary know that she wasn't in the mood by rolling her eyes at her. Soon after that the intercom came on and said that bus 251 was ready to be loaded with the passengers leaving for Texas. That meant me. I was so relieved I didn't think I could take Ida and Mama much longer. I got up, grabbed my luggage and headed for the bus.

There was a line so unfortunately I was delayed again. Mama and Ida moped toward the bus too, they were a sight to see. I handed my bags to the bus driver to put under the bus and I proceeded to give my final good-byes to everyone. In that moment I felt a big lump swelling in my throat. I had done so well up unto that point.

I tried hard to hold back the tears but they just came as they always did. Then I turned and gave Mama and Ida a hug. No words were spoken between us. However, just by seeing the tears in their eyes I felt all of the things they wanted to say but didn't know how.

I said nothing but I don't think it was because I didn't know what to say or how to say it. But I was just afraid of sharing my true feelings; afraid that they would not be validated or reciprocated.

One day as I sat in shop class, I could hardly concentrate because all I could think about were the last couple of pages that I read in Vileen's diary. I was hurting inside, I remember, that day when my sister left home, but I never knew the reason why she left, nor did I know how bad she longed to leave home. I hardly remember the accounts of that day the same way. I knew that I was always a handful but I never realized that I was unintentionally pushing my sister away from me. As I continued mulling over my actions, I kept wondering why I was so harsh, and so cold back then. I always had the attitude that no one ever cared including Vileen, I knew better now, but only too late.

"How could I make amends?"

The next spare minute I found, I picked up the tiny book once more and began to read;

Once I stepped up onto the bus I was determined not to look back but there was a brief hesitation on my part. I thought that perhaps the moment me and my family had shared could be a beginning and maybe it would work out for me to stay at home.

Suddenly I was swept back to reality when the bus driver beckoned me to move on. As the doors quickly shut behind me, I wanted to turn around and look back but I just couldn't. I continued walking forward down the aisle looking for an available seat one in which I could see all of the scenery.

The only one I found was in the aisle. A middle-aged white gentleman sat peering out of the window. I figured I would ease down beside him, hoping he wouldn't notice me. I was so tense I had my purse tightly gripped with both hands, my strap was still on my shoulder, my carrying bag was still in my hand.

About thirty-five minutes into the trip, the gentleman to my right turned to me and asked.

"What is your name?"

I told him that my name was Vileen.

"Where are you headed?" He asked.

I told him that I was headed to Texas.

He then asked me how old I was. By this point I wasn't sure whether or not I wanted to continue a conversation with this gentleman. I went ahead and told him that I was seventeen. He laughed and shook his head and said, "you are just a child, what are you doing traveling by yourself?"

I told him that I was on my way to school. Before the conversation went any further, I asked him his name. He said, "*my name is John and I have a daughter about your age but she is living with her mother in Georgia.*"

He also told me that he was recently divorced and he too was heading out to Texas to find a better job. He had gotten laid off of his job at some plant in Little Rock, Arkansas. Then with a deep sigh John briefly turned back towards the window.

I could see that he too was in pain and that perhaps he also was running from something. Just thinking about it brought tears to my eyes. He abruptly turned to me and asked me why in the world I was crying.

I told him that my tears represented all of the disappointment, frustration and the hurt that I had been through in my life as well as others who have been through the same or similar experiences. He sighed and then turned back around and began peering out of the window as if he really could relate to me.

I asked him why must we people go through all kind of trials and tribulations in life when ninety percent of the time none of it is a result of our own actions.

I then began to unveil bits and pieces of my life to John. However, I did not intend to tell this total stranger so much about me and my life, it just happened. It seemed as if once I got started talking I could not shut up for anything.

I must say that I can remember that at certain points during my ramblings I tried to stop—Lord knows I did—but the more I tried to stop the more I talked. John never said one single word to me. He just sat there and listened quietly and patiently. At least I thought he was listening. He kept peering out of the window *however, now it seems very possible that he might not have heard a word I was saying.*

He could have very well been lost in his own world, but I talked anyway and the more I talked the better I began to feel. I must have talked for hours because before I knew it we were in Dallas, Texas and I knew that the bus would be stopping soon. I gathered all my belongings so I would be ready to exit the bus.

John was still peering out of the window. I often wondered what was so entrancing about the window and just what images did it project in his mind. I also wondered just how that window would project me. I gently tapped him on the shoulder to alert him that we would be arriving at the station in a matter of minutes, and that perhaps he should gather his things.

He turned and looked at me cockeyed as if he didn't even know where he was. It was evident that his mind wasn't there and then after about a minute or so he became coherent and began to gather his things.

After he finished he wished me good luck on my journey and I wished him the same. When the bus stopped we both edged our way through the crowded bus station and then we went our separate ways.

Chapter Four

❧❦

On My Own

I would often read Vileen's diaries after lunch because it was quiet and most of my fellow inmates would take naps. I enjoyed the silent slumber times that I spent alone reading my sister's writings. They really gave me something to think about.

I started to see a pattern in her writings as time went on. These books were more than a mere diary. But in so many ways it was her story, it was her life, and as I read about her trip across country I began to see, hear and feel the things she wrote of as if I were there. Her writings were becoming so very real to me—maybe too real. I opened the book and continued reading where I left off.

After I got my luggage I went inside of the crowded bus station. It was much bigger than the one back home and a lot nicer too. They had small televisions hooked to the chairs where you could watch television while you waited for the bus. I then got in line at the ticket counter to verify my bus number. When I finally reached the front of the line I asked the attendant when bus number 771 would be leaving for San Antonio. He replied at 11:00 AM in a very rude monotone voice. I thanked him and I found a seat.

When I looked at the clock I realized that I had about forty-five minutes to wait. It was just enough time to grab something to eat and to go to the bathroom. As we had arrived at the bus station I noticed a small restaurant across the street. After I used the bathroom I walked over to see if the prices were reasonable. As I walked in the door I was taken back, the scenery reminded me of something out of a 1940's movie.

There were little yellow stools at the counter where you could eat and the booths were small and very decorative. There was an old juke box over in the corner. Since I only had a three dollar allowance per meal, after looking at the menu board I knew I did not have enough money to eat there.

I quickly walked back across the street to the bus station. Just as I was about to enter the door. I observed a vendor through the corner of my eye. I walked a little closer and noticed that he was selling hot dogs, chili dogs, and potato chips.

That man seemed to have a little bit of everything and the prices were very reasonable also, especially for a budget as small as mine. The hot dogs were fifty cents each. I got two hot-dogs, a bag of chips and a soda.

Then I journeyed back inside the bus station and I found myself a nice window seat as I began to eat my lunch. I sat there watching the traffic go back and forth, stopping and going, and then a sudden ere feeling came over me.

I was sure that I had been there before, perhaps in some other time even if it did only exist within my own mind. The scenery looked all too familiar and it reminded me, oh, so much, of the way things were back home.

There I was sitting miles away from home. Yet to my surprise the scenery was much the same and the people also were the same, they had different faces but yet they were all the same. Some of them even reminded me of people I grew up with back at home. As I sat and looked at the faces of the many people who sat there alongside of me, they all reminded me of someone or something. By then it was more than evident that people are people wherever you go.

I think it was a smile, a certain look, a mannerism or two. They all reminded me in some way or another. The cars and the streets were all the same. Yet on the opposite side of the coin I thought, we spend a lifetime trying to convince ourselves that we will never be like a certain person or there is no one else in the world like us. Meanwhile the very person that we are afraid of becoming is the person we already are, no matter how small the trait.

And that thought frightened me. Because if this were true then that would mean that I was just like Mama. It gave me chills and I didn't want to think about it anymore so with that thought I snapped back into reality. When I looked up at the clock, I had about eight minutes before the bus was due to pull out.

I thought it might be a good idea to head toward the bus, so there I went luggage and all. Although I didn't hear any announcement, I just figured somehow I might have missed it because I was in such deep thought. I hurriedly walked through the bus terminal, giving my luggage to the carry man and we began to load the bus.

This time I made sure I got a window seat right in the front row. I was ready to go and get on the road because fatigue was settling in. My body was on the verge of sheer exhaustion.

After everyone settled down and the driver shut the doors, we pulled off for our journey to San Antonio, Texas about 2:30PM.

I can hardly say that I remember what happened after that because before I knew what had hit me I had fallen into a deep sleep. I remember having this dream and in the dream I was sinking surrounded in a large body of water. I would go under and then I would come up again for air. I would hear the water splashing against the rocks as I went down again, struggling to stay afloat.

Then I was up again gasping for air. Somewhere along the way I caught a glimpse of two seagulls flying over head and then down again I went. Then up again I came and I caught a glimpse of a floating object about ten feet in front of me and then down again I went just fighting and kicking, choking on salty water. The sounds grew louder and then harder and harder. I began to flap my arms and kick my legs and then suddenly I heard a loud pop and that's when I woke up to find a balloon had burst in my lap. A little boy was hanging over the bus seat laughing at me. I wasn't laughing because it wasn't funny to me, he scared the life out of me.

His mother promptly apologized to me but I was still very uneasy to say the least. I settled back down into my seat and I began to think about the dream and its significance. The more I thought about it the more it seemed to come together.

The body of water that enveloped me probably represented the world out there and the constant struggle just to survive from day to day. The splashing against the rocks took on the form of a pendulum keeping track of every second, every minute, constantly reminding me that time was of the essence.

The seagulls served as a show of tranquillity that comes from time to time and then fades just as quickly. The floating object I figured must have represented hope and it gave me something to reach for, to strive for. It gave me a feeling of peace. This dream had really touched on some important issues in my life. The world, time, freedom, hope; I found it to be much more than coincidence. As the bus continued down the long highway, I decided to turn and take advantage of my window view.

Everything was so green-the trees, the grass-as I looked as far as my eyes could see all I saw was a lot of flat land. I sat there with the wind blowing through my hair and the fresh smell of damp air blowing in my face as I enjoyed the view.

Once again I found myself beginning to cry first one tear and then another and then a whole stream. It seemed as if I just couldn't help myself, I just couldn't figure out this fixation with the water and why it depressed me so and without another thought I scurried to perk myself up as the bus driver questioned to see if I was okay.

"Hello there, are you okay?" He asked.

I politely told him that I was fine. He then told me that things weren't as bad as they seemed. And that if I lived long enough to be his age, I would see that the things that people worry about the most are only temporary and in time they are forgotten and new trials arise.

I listened very attentively as he spoke but deep down inside I disregarded much of what he said. In an attempt to change the subject, I asked him how much further we were from San Antonio.

He replied, "about an hour." He then leaped back to the previous conversation.

"So why were you crying?"

"I do not want to talk about it, besides you might think it is stupid anyway," I said.

He still beckoned me to go ahead and tell him, assuring me that he would not think that it was stupid. Reluctantly, I went ahead and told him that water depressed me, that it made me cry.

He then laughed.

I must say that it really annoyed me. When he looked up in the rear view mirror and saw the expression on my face, he quickly stopped, but it was to late. The damage was already done.

"Please don't be angry with me," he said. "The laughter was merely my way of identifying with you." He went on to say that he too felt a bit of depression when it rained but he was certain it was not because of the rain itself; rather the emotions that the rain brought out of him.

He explained by saying that water was a part of Gods creation and that nature in and of itself gives us as human beings a sense of peace and the peace that we feel at that moment often allows us to experience emotions that we don't otherwise have the time to feel. As I began to think about what that old gray-haired man was saying, it slowly began to make sense to me. The rain and the water did give me a sense of calming peace, which allowed my innermost suppressed emotions to emerge.

I know now that the rain in its own way is healing. It gives me a brief moment to look at myself from the inside out. I can't remember much else that we talked about but I do remember that he was a very honest and sincere person.

About that time the bus driver alerted me that we were only ten minutes from San Antonio. At last I couldn't wait to get there. I looked over my left shoulder and saw tall buildings in a distance. The closer we got the clearer the buildings became. Within the next few minutes we were at the bus station. The scenery was all too overwhelming for me. As the bus came to a stop, I gathered all of my belongings together and prepared to vacate the bus.

I stepped off the bus and I headed for the ticket counter to see if anyone had arrived there from the program. The attendant informed me that no one had inquired to her knowledge. As I left the counter, I entered the seating area and noticed the time on the clock, we were ahead of schedule by about thirty minutes.

It wasn't until I sat down that I realized how exhausted I was. I also had a killer headache. As I sat there and took a look around it only made me feel sicker. There were so many people moving about and for a moment I thought that perhaps I had made the wrong choice.

Then again I thought, of all the choices I had, why in the world did I pick Texas. However putting all of that aside I knew that I had to make the adjustment because somehow, some way all of this had to work out.

There I was sitting right smack dab in the center of downtown San Antonio, Texas. I felt like a little goldfish in a huge pond. While I sat there I fumbled through my purse to try and find the letter with the school's telephone number and my counselor's name on it. By the time I looked up I saw a tall slender black lady talking to the desk attendant. I then saw the lady pointing my way.

I assumed the lady walking toward me was my counselor. I could see that she had some sort of name tag on. As she got closer I could see that it read—Janet Wright, New Hope Center.

She asked me my name, I told her my name was Vileen Ford, She then introduced herself and told me that she would be driving me back to the center. Ms. Wright helped me gather my bags and we headed for her car.

"How did you enjoy your trip?" She asked.

"It was all right."

She just smiled.

"Well, How do you think you will like Texas?"

"all right, I guess. But there are just so many people."

"Don't worry, you will get use to it." She said.

She said that Texas would grow on me after a while and that when she first moved here she thought the same thing. Ms. Wright told me that she was certain that after I'd adjusted I would like it too. Well, I was open-minded and I was sure that she was probably right.

It seemed like we drove for about thirty minutes before we reached the small facility. There was a lot of silence in the car that day. She could probably feel my uneasiness and hesitation.

We had entered a residential area, the neighborhood looked modest and at the end of the street I could see what appeared to be a small facility. As we got a little closer, Ms. Wright informed me that this would be my home for the two years or so.

She pointed out that across the street was the main campus for the outreach project and that is where I would be staying. I looked at her with a deep sigh and smiled, we pulled in front of the driveway and the car stopped at an oval building.

I gathered all of my things together and I made an attempt to get out of the car. But silly me, I wasn't aware that the car had automatic locks, which meant that Ms. Wright had to push a button to unlock the doors. Before she could do that, I was over there tugging and pulling on the door almost to the point of exertion.

"You can leave your luggage in the car for now until we have finished signing you in," she said. I turned and followed her into the building and down a long hall to a desk where a lady sat to whom Ms. Wright spoke. She told her that I was a new student and that she was there to help sign me in. We then went through

some double doors and to a big open room with quite a few young people like myself, they were all standing in lines. Ms. Wright asked me to wait a minute and while I was standing there this guy walked up to me.

"Hi," he said. "My name is Stanley."

"Hello, mine is Vileen."

"I just got here and I don't know anyone," he said. "You look like someone I would like to get to know."

I thought, what kind of line is this guy trying to run on me?

He went on to say that this was going to be his second year here and that if we ran into each other again for me not to hesitate to speak to him. By that time Ms. Wright had come back, she had a smirk on her face as she said, "I see you met Stanley." Then she told me to only believe half of what he said because he had a reputation around school for telling only half of the truth, half of the time.

I had about figured that much out by myself. Still there was something about him I liked. He had quite a sense of humor, or maybe it was the way he walked. Perhaps it was the way he wore his hair or his enchanting smile. We then proceeded to a table where Ms. Wright gave me some forms to fill out and I wrote my name on a roster.

Then we headed back outside of the building and to the car. As we were getting in the car she told me that I would be staying in Victory Hall and that there were a lot of new girls there like myself. We got in the car and drove less than a half a block. I thanked Ms. Wright for all of her help.

This time before trying to exit the car, I waited for Ms. Wright to push the button; believe me, it was much easier. She helped me get my luggage out of the trunk and we carried it up the stairs. There was a long hall and then there were twelve doors on each side of the hall.

She told me that I would be staying in room D3. As we entered the room a feeling of dismay came over me. I was overcome with emotions because everything was so different than what I was used to. The room was so small but yet at the same time it was cozy. Ms. Wright informed me that I had a roommate and that her name was Ramona.

She said that Ramona was probably downstairs in the game room and maybe after I got settled in I could take a look around the campus. About that time a tall slender brown skinned girl came beebopping into the room with a big smile on her face. In a loud chippery tone she said, "you must be my new roommate."

Meanwhile Ms. Wright interrupted us to say that she had a meeting to attend. She politely tiptoed out and closed the door behind her. Ramona began to giggle as she turned to me and asked me how I liked my new counselor. I assumed that she was sarcastically referring to Ms. Wright. I kind of shrugged my shoulders. In a silent way I was implying that I thought she was all right.

Mona gave me this funny look and said that's good and then she mumbled something under her breath. She then showed me where I could store my clothes and she helped me put them away.

After we finished she told me that she would take me and show me around the campus and introduce me to some of her friends.

I agreed so when we were finished I took a shower, changed my clothes and we went downstairs to the game room. It was a dim-lit building that stood off to the side of the laundry room. About twenty people were in there that day. It seemed pretty crowded to me considering the room's small nature but somehow we pressed our way through the rambunctious crowd.

It was still too crowded for me and I knew right then that this was not a place I would be visiting often. I was careful not to offend anyone; after all these were young people from not only some of the poorest cities but also the roughest cities in the country. And after all I was the new girl on the block and Mona hadn't been there too much longer, so we both were pretty much in the same boat.

We finally made it to the back of the room where Mona saw one of her friends. I just sat there and checked out the scenery as Debra and Mona talked. I have to admit that it wasn't quite what I had expected. Then again, I can't really say that I knew what to expect. Nevertheless I was there now and I had to make some adjustments. Somehow things would have to come together.

I was exhausted so I told Mona that I was going back to the room to get some rest. The moment I stood up and began to walk I could feel the sleep catching up with me. It seemed as if my body grew heavier and heavier. I could hardly make it up the steps. I was so relieved when I reached the room. I just flopped down on the bed and soon I was fast asleep.

The next thing I knew it was morning and I felt awful. I was so tired; I forgot all about calling Mama and Ida. After I got dressed, I went downstairs to see if I could find a telephone and to my surprise there was none to be found.

I then went inside the main building to ask them where I could find the nearest pay phone. Wouldn't you know it, the only one available for me to use was right outside the activity room. I hurried across the campus in hope of having access to the telephone but when I got there someone was already using it.

Therefore I just had to wait. That's when Stanley showed up, his mouth was running a mile a minute. He was talking about a program that the school was having and about ten other things, however nothing he said seemed of any importance.

"What are you doing out here so early in the morning?" He asked.

In a harsh tone, I told him that I was waiting to use the telephone and if he didn't mind he needed to mind his own business. About that time the girl that was on the phone hung up.

I then proceeded to make my call. Although I was anxious to call home I was also afraid. Even though I missed them, I didn't want them to know how homesick I was. But I knew that I had to call, and so I went ahead and dialed the telephone number.

The phone rang once or twice and then again my heart began to pound and the thought crossed my mind that maybe they weren't at home. Then to my dismay the phone stopped ringing and it was clear that someone had picked up the line. "Hello," I called out frantically and then I heard a frail distant voice reply on the other end of the phone saying "hello, who is this," and I replied; "hi, Mama it's me, Vileen."

From there on we just began to talk and talk. Mama sounded so different. I could even hear a touch of concern in her and Ida's voice as they told me that they missed me. We must have talked for about twenty minutes. Mama gave me a good run-down on everything that was going on in the neighborhood and then I began to feel as if I had been gone such a long time. When actually, it had only been a couple of days.

We soon ended our conversation with a solemn good-bye and that was it. I can't imagine why I was so fearful, but I had to admit that I really did miss home. It was all I had ever known.

As I read those words I began to cry. I too felt the sorrow that my sister felt. I began to think about my sister's quest for understanding of herself and the world. I also stopped to reflect on my life and where I was. I think that through her experiences I gained strength. I began to think about constructive changes I could make in my life such as how could I improve myself, my situation.

Living in a 12 by 12 cell was no kind of life for anyone. But I knew that like my sister I had to start planning, I had to start somewhere. For the first time I began to think about the day when I would leave prison. I made a list of things I could do to make my transition to the outside world easier. Once more I wiped the tears from my eyes and continued to read.

I couldn't give way to my tears, there were too many people around. Then out of nowhere came Stanley again, popping up in my face, asking me if we could resume our conversation. I told him that I did not recall having a conversation with him in the first place. I did, but I was just trying to get rid of him as fast as I could and he got the message. I then hurried back to my room and when I got there Mona was up and about. She asked me if anything was wrong. Immediately I replied, "no."

Then a big old tear drop gave me away and Mona replied, "so you're homesick." I denied it although I knew in my heart that she was right. I was too ashamed to let anyone else know it. She tried to console me but it did little good. I must have spent the next couple of days sobbing.

PS. Until tomorrow, better days ahead

Chapter Five

೧ ೫

A World Away

Soon I had learned to read in between the lines. Just as my sister had and adjustment to make, so did I. I also knew that there was much to be learned from her experiences and that she would come through for me no matter what, even if time did separate us.

I also knew that what she said from here on out had everything to do with me. I still don't quite understand how I ended up in a lifestyle of drug addiction. It always took me to a place of no return, but one thing I am certain of is that a change must come. Besides where else is there for me to go.

About that time a girl from next door came by my cell and asked me if I wanted to go the game room. I told her no. After I recovered from that interruption I picked up the tiny book and I began to read once more.

Dear Diary,

Today is March 12, 1987. And it has been some time since I have written you. I am beginning to adjust to school. It was the winter session before everything began to come together. I am doing well in all of my classes and I have plenty of friends. It almost seems too good to be true. Ms. Wright called me into her office a couple of days ago to ask if I would like to join a program called "TOUCH." This is an organization that focuses on the education and development of young people who had journeyed down the same or similar road as I had. I agreed to help out a couple of hours every week at the recreational center across town.

I knew that transportation was going to be a problem. Ms. Wright said that the school could put me on a work study program which would give me the extra money I would need to pay for bus fare to and from the center.

This program means a lot to me and I am willing to do a little extra work if it will make a difference in somebody's life. I left out of that office feeling so proud of myself and of the responsible decision I had made. The program starts the day after Easter. I am so excited I can hardly wait.

PS. Until tomorrow, brighter days ahead

The next entry started by saying:

Dear Diary,

Today is April 24, 1987. I've been so busy thinking about the program. It started this afternoon after my typing class. I hurried to the bus stop at the end of the corner. It was a little scary because it was in a rough neighborhood, although I know the neighborhood I came from was not much better. I was still uneasy, but I guess by it being a different city it will take me a while to adjust.

When we got in the building we were met by Mr. McCloud. He is the program's director. He explained that a lot of the kids there come from backgrounds similar to ours. He then gave us a piece of paper and asked us to write down why we volunteered to participate in the program, along with a list of things that we were good at. I was doing fine up until that point because I already had the answer to the first question, but it was the last one that really puzzled me.

What was I good at? I had to think long and hard because there wasn't any one particular thing that stood out among the rest. I guess Mona and me were the only ones who looked like we were having a really hard time. Mr. McCloud looked over in our direction and pointed his long slender finger at us and he said, "You two come over here. I am going to give you the music class." We both just stood and looked at each other with this dumbfounded look on our faces.

I didn't know the first thing about music, but Mona did. Lucky for us she had taken music and dance lessons when she was younger through a similar program in her home town. I looked at Mona and I shrugged my shoulders and she leaned toward me and whispered, "Don't worry about it; you'll be just fine." Mr. McCloud finished dividing the group into twos and told us what the rules were and what was required of us.

After the orientation he showed us around the building to let us see where we would be teaching. He also provided us with a

*list of students' names that had signed up for that particular
class. As I walked through those halls I began to feel real good.*

*Well, that was how the very first day turned out. When we
finally made it back home, we settled in and Mona and I
discussed just exactly what we wanted to accomplish in the class
by the time it was over.*

*Mona suggested that a musical would be a creative way to
depict life for the kids. We decided that we would let the kids
write their own words and we would help out on the music and
the dance steps. These are the best of times and I hope they will
last forever.*

> *PS: Until tomorrow, but having the time of my life*

Dear Diary,

*Today is May 15, 1987. Yesterday was gone and a new and
glorious day had dawned. I hadn't called Mama and Ida in a
while so I decided to give them a ring. When I called I let the
phone ring about ten times but no one answered. I figured I would
try back later in hopes that someone would be home. I gave little
thought to them not answering the telephone at the time.*

*After class Mona and I met back at the room to change so we
could get ready to go downtown to work with the kids. I was
scared. This would be the big day. Everyone met at the bus stop.*

After we got on the bus, It was quiet as if each of us was lost in his or her own world. The bus finally stopped at our destination. We exited single file, like docile little soldiers. As we walked in the doorway of the gym all I could see was dozens of faces peering at me. I had never seen so many faces in one place and in each face I could see the hope and the expectations behind their little eyes. I could hear all kinds of whispers and snickers from a distance.

I am certain the jeers didn't make me feel any more at ease. By this time reality was beginning to set in with us; we had taken on a big responsibility and it was not going to be an easy one. As I peered back across the crowd I could see that a lot of those great plans that I had stayed up planning the night before were not going to happen, not in this lifetime anyway, and most definitely not with this group of kids.

Mr. McCloud called us out one by one as he introduced us to our soon-to-be pupils. There was so much confusion. Kids were walking about, laughing, talking, doing their own thing. Mr. McCloud kept insisting that they sit down and then he turned to us and he smiled and said, "You see you've got your work cut out for you."

My first thought was to turn and run but I knew that I had made a commitment to myself as well as to the kids. No matter what, I had to stay.

We finally made it to our little room off the corridor from the main room. There we were at the center of attention as we took center stage with eighteen pairs of eyes staring at us.

Mona introduced herself and told them a little bit about her and then I did the same. Everyone of them was so very quiet and I will never forget the looks on some of their faces, there was a lot of different variations of the same thing-which was distrust. I guess that was the second or third year for most of them and in the previous two years their music classes had always been canceled for some reason or another. How could I really blame them?

The kids took turns telling a little bit about themselves and at times about each other while everyone got better acquainted. It made me feel so good inside to see those kids opening up and getting comfortable with their environment. We wanted our classroom to be a kind of safe haven from whatever was happening in their personal lives as well as ours.

It was plain to see that we had many different personality types. Christina talks a lot and Joshua seems as if he can really get on somebody's last nerve. Then there is Donna, she is so timid.

Yet all of them were products of the same or similar environment. But I must say the first day went rather well in spite of all of the mitigating circumstances. I think that each of us left there with a warm feeling inside because we understood the importance of giving something back no matter how little it was. Even Stanley looked like he had a serious and caring side to him for a moment.

It was about eight o'clock when we got home. Most of us had homework to do. Someone suggested that we all go out and get ice cream or something to treat ourselves but the majority decided that maybe it would be best if we saved it for another day.

When I got back to the campus instead of going straight to my room, I decided to stop at the telephone to try and call home again. I dialed the number and the operator came on and said that the number you have dialed has been disconnected or is no longer in service.

I thought that maybe I might have accidentally dialed the wrong number so I tried again but to no avail. The operator came on and once again said that the number you have dialed has been disconnected. I reluctantly slammed down the phone and I walked vigorously toward my room, as all sorts of things were going through my head.

Did they just up and move and not tell me? I paced the floor trying to think of some reasons why the telephone would be disconnected. None of the ones I came up with were quite good enough. It was about 11:00 o'clock when I decided to go down stairs to try the number once again but to no avail; the recording came on again.

I somehow mustered up enough strength to drag myself to my room and all night long I just laid there lifeless trying to think of a way that I could get in touch with Mama. Then I remembered her sister Sarah. I knew that she lived in Maine and that her last name was Brown. I made up my mind that I would get up first thing in the morning and see if I could call the operator and get a listing for her.

Dawn did finally come and I quickly arose and hurried to the phone. Someone was already using it and so I had to wait in line. I knew that this meant I would probably be late to my first class but I was willing to take the risk under the circumstances.

I dialed the number and the operator answered. I asked her if she had a listing for a Sarah Brown. She said that she had several. I told her to try the first one and then the recording came on and gave me a number. I hung up the phone and dialed it. The phone rang once and then again and then someone picked up on the other end.

"Hello, Hello," it was a male voice, I asked.

"Is this the Brown residence?"

He replied that it was and asked who did I want to speak to, I answered Sarah. He then informed me that no one lived there by that name. I hung up the phone, my spirit was shattered.

How in the world was I going to know which number was hers? I couldn't afford to call every Sarah Brown in the listings. I decided to try the operator once more. Again the operator said she had several listings. She asked me what street did my aunt live on and I told her that I did not know for sure. I asked her if she could please read off a couple of street names for me. I told her it was very urgent.

The operator began to read off the names of the streets, Palm, Jackson, Ray, Hebrew, Rockingham, and then suddenly I yelled— for her to stop. "Rockingham," I said, "yes, Rockingham." The operator put me through to that number, the telephone rung maybe one and a half times and then there was an answer.

The voice on the other end of the line sounded wonderfully familiar. It was so calming to me because now maybe at least I could put my worrying to rest.

I said, "Hello Sarah, this is Vileen."

"Hi! How are you doing?" She replied "I'm all right." I then told her that I tried to call Mama but a recording keeps coming on saying that the phone has been disconnected.

I asked her if she had heard anything from Mama. There was a pause and a sigh, and I didn't know what to think.

Then she said, "Vileen, your Mama has been having some hard times lately. Ida has gotten strung out on drugs and she is selling everything in the house; stealing money from your Mama and on top of all of that, your Mama found out that she is having trouble with her liver."

"Vileen," she said, I guess your Mama has drunk so much over the years until now her body just can't take anymore. The doctors told her that she has to quit drinking or it's going to be her life on the line. As she was talking, tears were just rolling down my face. At first I felt so sorry for Mama and then all of a sudden a feeling of anger came over me.

Sarah asked me was I going to be all right and I told her that I would but I knew that nothing was ever going to be all right as long as Mama wasn't right. I suggested that maybe it would be best if I went home to see if I could help get things straightened out.

Sarah pleaded with me to stay there and try to concentrate on my studies. She said that it was probably the best thing that I could do for Mama at that particular time.

Sarah was a heck of a persuader and before long I had agreed to her suggestion. With that we said our good-byes and I hung up the telephone. Sarah promised me that she was going to visit Mama that weekend to see if there was anything she could do. Although I did not like the circumstances I was more than relieved that I had made some kind of contact and I knew more than I did before I made the telephone call; it made me feel better.

When I looked up at the clock it was 11:00 AM and I knew that by that time my Accounting class was over but it was a day that I just had to miss. I hurried back across campus to Felly Hall, where my next class was to be held.

Somewhere along the way I ran into Mona, she asked me what was the matter and did I get everything resolved. I told her that I had gotten in contact with my aunt and she was going to visit my Mother this weekend. Mona replied; "that's good." I never bothered to go into details about Mama's drinking problem although we all knew that each one of us was there because we all came from broken homes. However, she let me know that she wished the very best for my family, and I thanked her for that.

This ended a long and exhausting day for me. The minute my head hit the pillow I was fast asleep. Sometime during the night I was awakened by a thunderstorm. The thunder would roll and then the lighting would flicker. The whole entire room was as bright as if it were noonday. Boom and then flicker, flicker and intermediately I would hear the rain just pour down, sounding like bacon sizzling in the frying pan.

I quickly pulled the cover over my head because I was afraid to see. When I finally mustered up the courage, as I pulled the covers down and tried to look out of the window. I found myself trapped in a trance peering out of the window.

Then it all started—it was inevitable I guess you could say. A big lump formed in my throat and my eyes began to get cloudy. I could not fight it any longer and the tears began to roll down one after another, and my thoughts quickly turned from my fear to all of the impending frustrations and problems that I was facing in my life. Some of everything crossed my mind. I thought about Mama and I thought about Ida. I thought about school and its uncertainty and then I began to remember what the old man had said. I began to say to myself, "healing, Vileen, healing," but before I knew it. I was really boo hooing. I must have cried myself to sleep that night because by morning my eyes were puffy and swollen.

It was another boring day at school and nothing out of the ordinary happened. I went to my classes and then to my work study job at the bookstore. The only thing that made any day extraordinary was when I went downtown on Wednesdays and Fridays to the center. I found that this had become my source of gratification.

———————

Dear Diary,

Today is January 4, 1988. It has been about eight months since we started the program and everyone of the kids have decided that we should do a musical for our final class project. Mona and I assigned everyone their parts. We decided that everything would be original—the characters, the scenery, and the music. We wanted the kids to write their own lines. We encouraged them and gave them as much support as we could.

Everything was going along fine and in the days and the weeks that had passed everything began to come together. We had finished all of the dialogue. Now all we had to do was to work on the music.

It was then when I noticed, little shy Rachel who was always humming and singing to herself. So I took her to the side and gave her the dubious task of helping me with the lyrics. The theme that the children came up with was, "To Show Me Love" and all of the lyrics centered around a day in the life of each or anyone of the kids. However, all of the scenes shared one common thread and that was one of pain and misunderstanding. But that day I found a talent that I never knew existed.

As we sat there diddle daddleing around, I began to write a line or two and it sounded good, real good to me. It was almost like they weren't even my words. I don't know where they came from—nowhere I guess—I just began to write:

> *All I have known is the way that things are,*
> *never understanding the reason why,*

always being to afraid to cry, can anyone
help the way that I feel? But with help I
know I can heal the emptiness inside,
the fear that keeps subsiding.

Can you dare to show me love?
Can you, will you, try and take the time, maybe we can
cross over the lines to reach out and find someone
who's been waiting there for you to show them love

And then I sat back and read what I had written and I reread it again and again. The more I read it the more it began to make sense. I knew that the next phase would be putting it to music. However that was Mona's department. We decided that we would work on the music more when we got back to the dorm. I left there that day with a great sense of accomplishment and a new found joy.

Everyone met at the bus stop and we all decided to go out and get some ice cream. Stanley knew of a little hamburger shop which was around the corner, so we all agreed to go there. We had so much fun last night; we laughed and talked about our students and the progress we had made with them.

Mona then told everyone that I had written a song. Everyone then begged me to recite a few lines for them. Stanley then said, he knew I could be good at anything I set my mind on. He went on to say that from the first time he laid eyes on me, he knew there was just something special about me.

I didn't pay him any mind because Stanely was a barrel of jokes most of the time and no one hardly ever took him seriously. Everyone then turned to each other as they began to smile and smirk. Stanley then moved his seat right beside mine. Mona then shouted, "is this going to be the beginning of something big?"

Everyone just laughed as I said no, not a chance. In that moment Stanley looked at me and smiled, and I smiled back. Yet, and still under my breath, I murmured, "not in this lifetime." We all finished up and headed back to the campus. Everyone said goodnight as we went on our way. But Stanley called me back and asked me if we could go out on a date next week.

I told him that I would have to see how things worked out. "Goodnight," I said. As he skipped off down the sidewalk like some big kid. Mona and I then headed up to our room. She couldn't wait to get there so she could find out what Stanley and I were talking about, but I stuck to my guns and I refused to tell her as I got dressed for bed.

Goodnight Mona, I said and she said the same and as I lay awake there in my bed I began to smile, because Stanley liked me but I couldn't see myself going out with a tall, skinny, goofy boy? He was just such a clown; always talking, but I had to admit that he was kind of cute and he did seem to have a sensitive nature about him. Perhaps I would take him up on his offer one day, I thought. All and all I had to admit that everything was really going great.

Dear Diary,

Today is January 15, 1988. Just two weeks ago I was the happiest I had been in a long time. But, yesterday there was a student body meeting in the gym and we were all informed that due to new legislation the funds for our school program had been cut almost in half.

Therefore, the food and book allowances that we had been receiving would be sharply decreased. I was in a state of shock, it just came out of nowhere without any warning. I was so angry! Why hadn't anybody said anything before this? They knew all of our circumstances after all; that is why we were all here in the first place. All I could think of was what am I going to do? The administration also informed us that the staff was going to be cut nearly in half and that they had to decrease the student body by about ten percent in order to stay afloat.

Mona looked at me and I peered back at her and in our eyes one could see the level of anxiety that began to consume us. That was the last of what I heard because the other words that followed just went whizzing over my head. I had heard all I wanted to hear. Mona and I comforted each other on the way back to the room.

The minute we got in the door I threw myself on the floor and began to cry out a loud, why? Why? And Mona just laid there looking at me. I then asked her what was she going to do and she replied; that she was going to do the same thing she had done before she had come into the program. I asked her what that was and she said she worked two jobs and taught music on the side. She said that if things got worse, she would go back and do that.

I began to question how she changed directions so abruptly and all of a sudden this jovial hearted girl jumped up off of her bed and into a rage. She told me that I didn't know anything about her and about her life. I thought how dare she even make such a statement because every single one of us that were here were in the same or similar situation. What gave her the right to think that she was any different than anybody else including me.

She began to go on about how her mother left her at birth and she was raised by her aunt, who was a parent, who physically abused her. My reply was, "AND." Before I knew what hit me she had hauled off and slapped me. I must say that I wanted to slap her back, but I knew that it wouldn't have done any good.

Instead I told her that both of us grew up in abusive homes and that as adults were going to have to make a conscious decision to change our lives. Then I said, "besides I am sick and tired of fighting verbally as well as physically and I am not going to fight you." She just looked at me as she busted out crying and then we embraced.

The administrators stressed to us that things were not going to change much but in spite of what they said I began to brace myself for the worse.

PS. Until tomorrow, holding my bucket of sorrows

Chapter Six

∞

No Life For Me

I had finally finished book number four and just in time I might add, I stood up and stretched my legs out to get relief. It was dinner time and so I washed my hands and headed to the mess hall.

I did not eat much. I can distinctly remember because I was so into the books. I couldn't help but want to know what would happen next. Then I found myself worrying about the same things that troubled my sister. I found myself wishing that things would work out for her.

I had to constantly remind myself that these events were in the past and had already unfolded; and there was nothing I could do to change them. I often didn't eat much so I could hurry back to my cell in hopes of having just a few more hours to read. Then I would sit down on that tiny cot and began to read.

BOOK #5

Dear Diary,

Today is April 7, 1988. Yesterday was so hectic, there was confusion everywhere. Rumors were out that there would be a meeting in Felly Hall at 3:00 PM, I began to prepare myself for the worst. We knew that this was going to be the big day.

Mona and I got there about 2:30 PM, we sat there with the other students speculating on exactly what they were going to say and how they were going to say it. Then the time came for the announcement. I saw Ms. Wright and the other counselors lining up across the stage and the teachers followed them.

It was more than apparent that before one word was spoken we all knew just what the verdict would be. I remember looking around and seeing so much gloom and then Dr. Paul came to the podium and began to speak to us. He told us that each of us was special and that we were some of the brightest and most talented young people he'd ever had the privilege of working with.

He went on to say that sometimes no matter how wonderful and great things seem they must come to an end and sometimes in the process people end up suffering. Dr. Paul said that the school would be closing due to lack of funding.

After he said that the students became belligerent and some yelled out obscenities, but I just sat there. I could see the sorrow in the faces of those who remained. After the meeting was over, a lot of us just sat there in a state of shock. Some of us didn't have anywhere to go back to and others did not want to go back home.

But me, I don't have anywhere to go either; at least that is how I feel right now. Perhaps it's because there is nothing back home, no jobs, no opportunities, none at all. I know that no matter what I have to stay.

Mona and I finally made it to the room, she looked at me and asked. What are we going to do?

I replied, "I am going to stay here and find a job." We agreed that we would stay in Texas, get an apartment and somehow work on going back to school.

> *PS. Until tomorrow, though I see troubles on ahead*

Dear Diary,

Today is May 2, 1988. It's a new day for Mona and me. We have formed a sort of bond as sisters. I can't help but see the resemblance to my old childhood friend, Sheila. Mona and Sheila share the same likeness of spirit. Mona is a little older than I am so she is more like a big sister to me and I think that we might be the very best of friends.

I finally feel that the gap has been bridged between us and after all of the catastrophes that have come up I am just thankful that we have each other to lean on. I guess that we are both lucky. Today when I went to my mailbox I received a brown envelope; it looked very official and it was then I knew that this was the letter I had been dreading. I haven't dared to open it for fear of reality setting in.

The committee tried to help a handful of the most desperate ones relocate to other schools, other locations. But we are one of the last ones left here. It is one of the most hardening things to see everything on the campus being closed down. It's so depressing. The little club house that use to be the happening place-well, it's empty now. Books are being packed up, there are boxes everywhere.

Dear Diary,

Today is June 3, 1988. The last few weeks here have been really rough because I feel as if I've been caught up in a nightmare. It's hard to sit by and watch my plans die right in front of me, but there isn't anything I can do about it. I have already made up my mind that I am going to stay.

"But how am I going to break the news to Mama?"

"After all, I have gone through so much trying to get here. Should I now turn around and go back?" I know that Mama will be disappointed at the school closing, but I also know that she will be expecting me to come back home.

However, it is not about to happen because there is nothing back home for me. I know in my heart that this will turn out to be a much better place for me in the long run.

Today I took out the letter I received several weeks ago. The addresser was the Young Adult Program Board of Directors. I'd finally decided to open the letter, oddly enough it read;

Dear Student,

We are sorry to inform you that due to a lack of funds for the program, we will no longer be able to render you service as of August 17, 1988. After I read that I balled the piece of paper up and threw it in the trash. Then a feeling of closure came over me. Any hope that I might have had was now put to rest for good.

This afternoon we began to pack. I know I have to call Mama but I want to make it the last thing I do before leaving school. There are only a few people remaining on campus and the mood is pretty somber.

As I continued to read, so much anguish filled my heart. I was beginning to understand her plight for success, for freedom. I was beginning to see what made her such a relentless pursuer of dreams, of goals. As I read on about the trials that she faced, never once did she mention quitting in her writings. As I sat and thought about myself and who I was, I wondered what made me choose a path so very different from hers in spite of the fact that we were raised in the same environment.

What made me so very different from her?

Was it a choice or was it a trait?

But I also knew that none of that mattered now and so I continued to read on.

We all scurried to make some kind of living arrangement. Some of the kids started looking for jobs around town. Mona and I began doing the same. Hope was really beginning to seem dim because no one was calling.

We must have put in about twenty applications when we finally got our first call from a fragrance company; they had several openings and were in the process of expanding. Several of the girls from the school got jobs there. They only paid minimum wage but we all had plans of roommating and finding a second part-time job if the need arose.

Mona and I found an apartment on the east side of town near Hill Top Acres. It is a small two-bedroom apartment; that is all we can afford right now. The rent is $285 per month plus a $200 dollar deposit but to our surprise the landlord waived the deposit. Otherwise I don't think that we would have ever had enough money saved in time to rent the apartment.

Dear Diary,

Today is July 5, 1988. Mona and I moved out of the school dormitory. I know that we are young and naive; yet we are determined that we will single-handedly overcome incredible odds no matter what. And having each other to lean on really helps.

Finally the time had come when I had to call Mama. I really didn't want to worry her since I knew that she had not been in good health. I attempted to dial the number but I just couldn't bring myself to make the telephone call.

I told myself that I would try back later after we had gotten all settled into the new apartment. It wasn't until evening when I finally got up the nerve to call Mama. The first time I dialed, no one answered the telephone; the second time I dialed someone answered on about the sixth or seventh ring.

I started out by making general conversation and then slowly changed the subject by saying that there had been some changes at the school. For some reason I could not find the words to get the rest of the sentence out.

I then began to perspire heavily. Mama, I said. The school is closing due to lack of funding and me and my roommate have moved off campus. But it wasn't until I heard the anxiety in her voice that I assured her there was nothing to worry about. My only concern was convincing her that everything was going to be okay.

I could hear her coughing terribly on the other end of the telephone. She sounded awful but she assured and reassured me that she was fine. I wonder if she wasn't doing the same thing I was doing—lying for peace of mind sake. Perhaps we were just fooling ourselves. After we had finished convincing each other that everything was going to be all right the conversation soon ended.

Later that afternoon we all got together and went back down to the recreation center to tell the kids about our misfortune. However, after we got there we didn't have the heart to tell them that we wouldn't be coming back. Besides we wanted to show them that someone did care about them. We wanted to be some kind of role model for them. And the best way to do that would be to finish what we had started.

The children already had all of their lines together and all we needed to do was to finish the lyrics. Mr. McCloud had a meeting at the end of our session to give us words of encouragement and to commend those of us who decided stay in spite of the circumstances.

I finally finished my song, which gave me a sense of pride and accomplishment and it really sounded good to me. The date of the recital was set for the following Saturday. Mona and I stayed up late the night before trying to put the finishing touches on all of the lyrics and the music. We finally finished about 2:30 AM and I was exhausted. We know that our reasons for staying are different and yet they are all the same. We genuinely care about what we are trying to do and understand the meaning behind our actions.

Dear Diary,

Today is July 13, 1988. Yesterday was the big day and the show went on as planned. Everything went so smoothly and everyone enjoyed the program. After the program we all had a get together to say our final good-byes to those who planned to leave Texas. That was the last time I saw Stanley. And that was the last of the Young Adults Program.

Its been three months now and all of the students seem as if they were just mere fragments of this puzzle of mine left somewhere way back in time. I must say that those were some of the best days of my life with memories that I will cherish for a lifetime.

Well, everyone has left except Mona and me. We share a small two-bedroom apartment. It is not in the worst neighborhood, but it is far from the best also. The apartment is furnished with old antique-looking furniture and for the most part it looks, okay. We have been working for a couple of months now on the assembly line at Mitchell's fragrance company. Although the job is mundane it pays the bills and puts food on the table. We work hard and eventually we will get promoted up the line.

The company owns a small cosmetic store and to work there would be a dream come true; to be Cosmetic Representative for the company is our goal. However, in the meantime we are doing what we have to do. We go to work on time and we do our job well. We pay our bills, besides what else can anyone ask of us.

———

Dear Diary,

Today is November 15, 1988. Its been sometime since I have written you there have been so many changes over the last couple of months but I'll just have to fill you in. About six months into my new job a representative came down to recruit for the cosmetic store. That day everyone had makeup on and wore their best clothes. Everyone was so nervous—there had been talk for weeks about someone coming down. Mona and I felt we had a good chance of getting selected since we had been on the job a lot longer than most of the other employees.

The representative talked with our supervisors. She then selected about twenty people to interview. They told us that they would call those individuals to set up appointments later on in the week. The anticipation was just killing us. I felt that we both had very good chances after all they were hiring ten people. So as the days and the nights passed we waited anxiously for an answer.

Tuesday morning the telephone rang and it was Ms. Bright, the representative from the cosmetic store. I was the one who just happened to answer the telephone.

"Hello," I said. "May I speak to Mona Guereo."

"Yes," I said. "Could you hold for one minute?"

Mona came to the telephone. I could hear the excitement in her voice and I knew that she had gotten the interview I was very happy for her but still a certain sadness filled my heart.

I was heart broken because I knew that I'd worked just as hard as anyone else if not harder. So the next day instead of going to work Mona went on her interview, it was lunch time when she stopped by to tell me that she had gotten the job.

At first I was angry with her because I felt as though she had somehow betrayed me. But how could I blame her for taking the job, I thought. The pay, the hours and the environment were better. Yet I still don't understand why I did not qualify for the position, and why I wasn't even considered for an interview. These and many other questions continue to puzzle me.

————

Dear Diary,

Today is March 1, 1989. It has been a couple of weeks and my job performance has gone down the drain. Work just isn't the same and besides, my best friend is gone.

In the next few months Mona received another promotion and this time she was promoted to department supervisor; when she came home and told me I was so happy for her. I really was even though there was a small part of me down deep inside that resented everything she was accomplishing, because I wanted it to be me.

But instead there I was trapped in this nowhere factory job and the other side of the fence looked so much better. As the weeks began to pass the resentment increased and I grew bitter; and soon it became ugly, very ugly, it was the rawest form of envy I believe I had ever seen.

The next few weeks were pure hell we bickered constantly. I blamed Mona for everything, even her new-found success. I was constantly searching for something to break the tension. Then one Saturday I guess it was about 12:30 PM when I received a telephone call from my Aunt Sarah. I remember feeling shocked to hear from her and then as I listened closer I could hear trembling in her voice as she said.

"Vileen, your mother is in the hospital and she is very ill. We need you to come home."

Somehow I mustered up the words to ask what was wrong and she said that she had cancer of the liver. That was the first time I had ever had any direct dealings with Cancer. She then told me the details. Although I must say that I cannot remember another word she said after that.

I told her that I was on my way and hung up the phone. The tears came as they always did but this time I just could not stop. Mona asked me what was wrong and I began to tell her that my mother was ill and I had to return home.

"Do you have enough money," she asked.

"No," I replied.

"Here,"she said as she went up under her mattress and handed me a wade of crumpled up bills.

The next day I made arrangements and started on my journey back home. As I sat there, riding on the bus I found myself reliving parts of the ever reminiscent past. Thoughts of Mama just plagued my mind. Some of them were of happy moments and others weren't so happy. Nevertheless the tears did try and come but I struggled and fought with myself to maintain composure.

As I continued reading I began to cry for my sister. Because I too was upset about Mama's health. But I didn't recall the accounts the same way. To be truthful I didn't recall them at all. I knew that I was probably somewhere getting high or hanging out with my friends and getting in trouble. Soon I realized that not only would I have to confront my relationship with my sister but I would also have to give account for my relationship with my mother.

I knew that it was going to be hard because so many of the painful memories I never experienced. Because there was always another high waiting to save me, but who was going to save me now? I thought. I could feel so much fear starting to brew inside of me. But I knew that I had to read on so I grabbed some toilet tissue and I continued to wipe my eyes as I read.

The journey back home seemed even longer than the journey there. Every place we stopped became significant to me. I picked out a certain spot, a certain monument, to always remind myself that I had been there. I guess that somewhere amidst the inner-

most recesses of my mind I knew that I probably would never return.

Finally we pulled into the bus station at about two or three o'clock. I got off of the bus, picked up my luggage, and waited inside the terminal for someone to pick me up. I must have sat there for about two hours before anyone came. When out of nowhere I saw a familiar face, it was Ida and I guess one of her boyfriends.

All of a sudden it felt as if I was swept back into that old familiar scene. I looked around me as I rode in the back seat of the car. I could see that everything was the same as it always had been and it really disappointed me.

I thought that perhaps the town itself had changed, or some of the people who live here, but everything and everyone is still the same. The same old wino's and prostitutes are standing on on the same corners. It is all the same old, same old. I don't know why but for some reason I was expecting a big change. I guess it's because I feel like I've changed so much.

Ida, I think she must have been the biggest disappointment to me because all that I had done in life, walking the straight and narrow and leaving home at a young age has had absolutely no affect on her.

I thought that by me leaving home and trying to better myself that I would be an inspiration to her. I feel like all I have tried to do has been in vain. As I took a look at the clothes she was wearing and the way she talked and her mannerisms, I knew that she was not following in my footsteps and that the path that she had chosen was her very own.

I knew that ultimately she would be the one who would have to pay for what she had done. It was hard for me to swallow, but what could I do?

My heart began to break as I read how Vileen felt about me but I knew that she was right. All I could do was to keep wiping the tears from my eyes as I read.

As we entered the old neighborhood I began to ask about old rivals. The journey back home was a very moving, emotional experience for me. We pulled in the driveway and I could see other cars parked alongside the house. Even the house had changed dramatically it seemed as if everything looked more run down. There was trash and old rusted tools out on the front lawn and the shutters were falling off the house.

I then turned and asked Ida who had been keeping up the house since Mama had been ill and she said no one. I fought hard to hold the tears back. It angered me so much to see that the house I grew up in had become such a hideous place to come back to. I knew that I did not grow up in a perfect family but home was still a special place to me and as far as I am concerned it always will be.

We shuffled our way through the mess and into the house. There must have been ten to fifteen people crammed in the front room, Ida introduced them to me. They were some of Mama's friends, from the treatment program at church.

I asked her where was Sarah and she told me that she was at the hospital with Mama. I decided that I would wait until later to go to the hospital. After I went to my room and got my stuff settled in I decided to get something to eat. It had been a long while since I had gotten a decent meal. People had brought over so many different kinds of food; I loaded my plate with cabbage, greens, sausage and black-eyed peas with corn bread.

After I finished eating I talked Ida into taking me to the hospital. I did not want to go but everyone was expecting me to. So I guess I had no choice. Perhaps I was afraid of what I would find and maybe, just maybe, I couldn't or wouldn't be able to deal with it.

Besides, I didn't want to remember Mama as being sick. I wanted to remember her just the way I always had, as a healthy young woman. Even as I was thinking that, I knew that it was far from the truth because Mama was rarely sober, and although at times she looked healthy on the outside she was probably dying on the inside.

By the time I arrived at the hospital it was about 5:30 PM and as I entered the hospital room nothing could have ever prepared me for what I saw. It was just awful and heart wrenching. She was asleep, I thought until Sarah told me that she had slipped into a coma the night before. I immediately became very angry because no one had told me. If they had I could have at least *prepared myself for the situation. After all I was looking forward to talking with her about Texas. There I was faced with not being able to talk to her—not then, maybe not ever—and that was very hard for me to swallow. As I stepped closer to the bed I could see her eyes begin to flutter. Instantly hope began to fill my heart and then Sarah told me that it was just a reflex.*

This caused me to stop and think about a lot of things but most of all it forced me to reevaluate my relationship with Mama. As the weeks began to pass I spent hours upon hours talking to Mama singing to her, and at other times just sitting and gazing at her, trying to make the situation into a bad dream.

PS. Until tomorrow, I'm still hoping for the best

———————

Dear Diary,

Today is June 5, 1989. I know that I don't write you as often as I use to, but my life has been very hectic lately. Months have passed and the doctors think Mama might die in the next few weeks. It is hard for everyone in the family to swallow.

Sarah and I are the only ones who continue to go and visit Mama at the hospital. Ida wants to pretend that none of this is happening and that perhaps it isn't real. I guess she just wants to hide, well so do I. But I just can't; someone has to be there for mama no matter what.

We have all begun to prepare ourselves for the worst. People from the church around the corner are constantly bringing food and all sorts of things; they are very supportive.

One day when I was visiting Mama in the hospital while straightening up her things I opened the night stand drawer to put something inside, when I stumbled upon a black leather Bible. I started to close the drawer but then I opened it again. I pulled the Bible out and I sat there for a moment and began to think about all I had ever heard about the book I held in my hands. That day began a quest for knowledge for me; one like I had never known before.

All of the Bible verses from vacation Bible school began to come to my remembrance. Verses about Jesus and his disciples and the miracles that they worked here on earth. Then I opened the book and I began to read;

John 14:6, KJV

"I am the way, the truth, and the life, no man cometh unto the Father but by me."

I sat down in the chair next to Mamas' bed as I began to read the pages aloud beginning from Genesis. Everyday that I would go and visit I would read a little bit more. Soon I began to find a certain peace in it all and for some reason I always felt that perhaps Mama could hear every word that was being spoken around her. I had been coming and reading to her, for about three weeks when I came upon this scripture. It read;

John 3:16, KJV

"For God so loved the world that he gave his only begotten son that whosoever believeth in him should not perish but have everlasting life."

After I read that verse I stopped and I reread it over and over again. I began to read in a audible voice where before I had been almost whispering so as not to wake the lady across the room from Mama. Each time I read it, it began to have more meaning to me. I ended up hovering over Mamas' bed and yelling "you hear that, Mama, did you hear that?"

I read the verse once more, Mama just laid there; there was no response. Then I looked again and I saw one solemn tear rolling down Mamas' face and then I was certain that she had heard me. Then came a stream of tears and I began to hug and kiss her.

All of a sudden I felt warm on the inside and it made me feel calm and at peace. I was certain that everything was going to be all right now. That night I couldn't wait to get home. I called everyone and told them about my experience. Mama was going to get better I just knew it. Before I went to bed that night I prayed a special prayer for Mama's recovery.

The next morning I woke up; in a great mood. I got dressed, cleaned the house, went to the store, and ran some errands. I couldn't wait to get to the hospital to spend time with Mama. So I decided to go an hour earlier than usual. When I got there nothing seemed out of the ordinary.

As I got off of the elevator and turned toward the corridor, I could see a lot of commotion going on down the hall. I began to walk faster and the closer I got the more I did not want to believe that they were going in and out of Mamas' room. When I got to the door a nurse stopped me and told me that I couldn't go in.

I told her that I was Ms. Ford's daughter. She politely asked me to have a seat outside in the hall. Then she proceeded to tell me that Mama had died. I began to scream and cry frantically, it can't be so—it can't be so because just yesterday she was doing so much better.

I asked them if I could see her. I still thought that they had made a terrible mistake so as I entered the room I slowly edged my way toward the bed. The machines were all turned off and everything was so quiet.

I could see a sheet had been pulled over her head, so slowly I reached my hand out and pulled it back. Her lips looked ashy and there was no doubt that she was dead. I could still see a tear that had dried up on her cheek.

I threw myself over her cold, pale limp body as I cried and screamed "why?," loudly. About that time Sarah entered the room and helped me to my feet. She tried to pull me away but I just kept saying; I just want to sit with Mama a little while longer.

She began to struggle with me because she knew that we had to go. As I was leaving I caught a glimpse of the night stand and there was the Bible we had read the day before. It was still open laying face down. I went back and picked it up and read the verse that was highlighted. Then I closed the book and clenched it tightly in my arms as I was escorted out of the room. That little black book means the world to me because it was the last thing that Mama and I shared together here on this earth.

After we made it a ways down the hall, Sarah told me to sit down for a minute because she had to talk with the doctors before we left. *I sat there for about thirty-five minutes in that cold terrifying place before she was able to take me home.*

Chapter Seven

∞

In Search Of Something

I stopped and closed the tiny little blue book as I thought about the events which had just unfolded. It was a horrible thing to read, to experience, even if it were second hand. I finally got up determined to get some rest, but none came that night or the next couple of nights that followed. Finally on the afternoon of that third day I resumed reading.

On the way home I never spoke a word to Sarah and she never spoke to me. When we pulled up into the driveway, we saw that Ida was home.

Sarah said, "I'll tell her," which was fine with me, because I barely had enough strength to make it to the house. I was in a total state of shock. I often wonder why they didn't admit me to the hospital that night. I was truly a wreck.

The next couple of days I don't know how I made it through. I wasn't eating much of anything and I just lounged around the bedroom all day. Thursday finally came and it was the day of the funeral.

I knew that if I could just make it through the funeral that maybe I could start rebuilding my world, my life. The funeral was a short and simple service. Quite a few people were there and a lot of them I did not know. The Pastor said a few words and then each family member placed a carnation on the casket.

I held up pretty well through the funeral. The next couple of weeks passed without me even acknowledging them. I had lost all concept of time. I would just lounge around the house all day.

One day a lady from the church down the street stopped by to check and see how we were doing. I guess that my appearance said it all because when I answered the door I was still in my pajamas and my hair was in rollers. I looked awful and I was really embarrassed. She invited me to go to church with her and she also told me that they were hiring at the local mall. She said her niece was a manager at a store there. I thanked her for her concern, her invitation and her suggestion.

It seemed like a month went by before I started coming around. I went over to the new store in the mall and got a job as a sales clerk. I believe that was part of what started me on my way to recovery. As I became more aware of my surroundings I began to try to piece things together. I knew that Mama had been sick but I just had to come to some kind of understanding as to why she died. It was the only way for me to make peace with myself, for myself. I felt as if God had betrayed me and had snatched Mama away from me.

I could not comprehend it. Everyday for the last three weeks that Mama was here on this earth I did nothing but read the Bible to her day and night. I prayed to God on several occasions and it seemed as if God had answered my prayers.

That last day Mama had gotten a lot better. But now I was back to square one with religion and the Bible; it remained a complete mystery to me. I vowed that I would find the answer someday. Life in Kentucky went on as usual except now I was having a real problem adjusting to living with Ida.

At times I felt like it was easier when I was in a state of depression because I hardly knew that she was around. Her life style and her friends were too much for me to handle. She wanted to have friends over all hours of the night, playing loud music, smoking, cursing and carrying on. Ida was as strong-headed as ever. If I said anything to her it meant a fight for sure.

And so many times I said nothing because I knew all to well what the end result would be. It really hurt me for us to fight because I realized that we were the only family that either of us had left. Often I would try to make her see that, but for some reason she just couldn't grasp it.

Slowly but surely life began to move on for me and then one Sunday I decided to attend the church service down the street. It had been a long while since I had been to church and I hadn't picked up a Bible since Mama's death.

That Sunday the Pastor preached about redemption and how Jesus died so that we could live and about the importance of sanctification. It really started me to thinking, why would someone I did not know give their life for me. I knew of the life Mama had lived up until the day she died and I wondered just where did Mama go, did she go to heaven or hell?

The next day I went to the cemetery to visit Mama, when I arrived at the grave site, I had all intentions of making peace with myself as well as with Mama. But as I began to talk to Mama there that day I found myself trying to understand why she died in spite of the fact that she was trying to clean up her life.

But then I remembered what the lady from church had said and I thought perhaps she was right. Maybe by me going to the hospital everyday and reading the Bible to Mama, I was merely a vessel by which God allowed her to find salvation. I honestly believe that somewhere and at sometime while I was sitting there reading to her she accepted Christ into her life as her personal Savior.

As I had read to her each day I just knew that she heard and was understanding me. I often think that those tears running down her face were an expression of her joy on the inside. Because she had finally made peace with herself, even though the next day she died. I feel that my prayers were answered and that God knew how to work things out for the best.

PS. Until tomorrow, In search of the truth

Dear Diary,

Today is January 8, 1990. Now and then I feel like I am right back where I started. I set out on a journey to get out of this town *and here I am still working in a dead end job struggling just to make it. I guess that's why I always wanted to get away so bad.*

Then one morning I woke up and decided that enough was enough, I was sick of the mode I had fallen into and it was most definitely time for a change. Still I knew there was little chance now of me ever leaving Kentucky.

Ida was there and I was all the family she had, so I decided I was going to find a new job something I enjoyed doing, something that made me feel good about myself. I set out telling friends and co-workers about my new found revelation and they all had the same basic response. Vileen, the job you have now is a good one. It pays the bills and is better than a lot of other jobs in this town.

I don't know why I was so surprised when I didn't get the support I wanted. I had heard all of the things they were saying over and over again but I was convinced in my heart that it just wasn't true. I had always felt that people got exactly what they expected to get out of life; therefore they should never be disappointed. I made up my mind once again to embark on some unheard of endeavor to find a dream and perhaps that would lead me to finding myself.

Every Sunday I would go and pick up a paper from down the street at Mr. Johnson's store. I would run home to see if there was anything in the paper that particularly interested me.

Weeks went by and I didn't have a clue as to what I wanted or even needed to do. I decided that maybe I needed to aim my search more toward learning about myself-my likes, my dislikes and what kind of person I was. I sat down one day after work and

I began to describe the environment that I felt most comfortable in and I was surprised at how much I was beginning to learn about myself.

Then one day I woke up with a great idea; I decided a marketing job was the job for me. I was a determined little person; once I set my mind on something it was going to happen. So I started applying for every sales job I knew about.

At first it seemed like my chances were slim since I didn't have any previous sales experience but then I got a call from a telecommunications company. They wanted me to come in for an interview. I was very nervous but once I got there the interview took every bit of five minutes or less and they hired me on the spot. I was so excited and I felt great that day. I just knew that was the career for me and that things were going to be very different from then on.

Later I went out and bought some new clothes for the new job and I took Ida out to dinner that night. I was having my first taste of joy since Mama had passed and it made me feel pretty good. Besides it came just in the nick of time, my birthday was only two days away. It seemed as though everything was coming together for me.

Around Christmas I started my new job. Management told us our sales would probably be higher than usual because of the holiday season. I knew that being a telecommunications sales person most definitely was not the most glamorous job. But it was a start.

The first few weeks were great but then one of the entry-level managers on the job began to make passes at me. And when they weren't reciprocated he really began to give me a hard time. I think that for sometime my spirit was dampened because of the experience he put me through. But nevertheless I was as determined as ever to go on.

The job was going okay other than that but I just knew that this job was not the one for me. I also knew that I did not have a lot to choose from in such a small town. Once again I began to dream about moving back to Texas.

I often wondered what had happened to Mona and Stanley and had they been successful in their endeavors. Although Mona and I had our share of problems she was really like a sister to me and I will always think of her as such.

Mother's day was about two weeks away and my depression was starting to really set in. I had made plans with Ida to go out to dinner at a little restaurant about three blocks away from the house. The dinner was fine but something was missing; it was painfully obvious that Mama wasn't there, but to me it was much more than that.

Somehow I managed to make it through dinner, it was so awkward. I felt as though I was having dinner with a total stranger. The face was familiar but that was all. It was more than apparent that Ida was high. After dinner Ida went over to one of her friends house and I got in the car and went for a drive. I often found that when I was upset or needed to do some problem solving, I would take a nice long drive and It would always ease my conscious.

I had to read that last paragraph once more, because it felt like a dagger twisting inside of me as my sister spoke of me in such a way. I remembered the dinner that Vileen was describing but I hardly remember me acting so badly. But she was right, I was high.

As I drove down Independence Blvd., it was as if my whole life began to flash before my eyes. Just the thought that I was going somewhere and I was in control of where and how far I went gave me a sense of power, a sense of control.

I was also troubled and very weary I wondered what I could do to get out of my rut I had fallen into. Ida and I were all we had left and I could see that each day I was losing her to drugs, to the streets and as a young woman my resources were limited. I did the best I could but it just wasn't working and I had to do more, I just had too.

Going a little further down the road, I saw an old bar on the corner. I decided to stop in to see what was so enticing to Ida that it would be more important than her own family. When I got in the door I saw a smoke filled room with people stacked on top of each other like sardines, drinking and dancing. This guy came up to me and asked if he could buy me a drink. I frankly declined because he smelled like a brewery. It just made me sick to my stomach. As I sat there at the table with him for about ten minutes looking around and observing the scene. To my surprise I found it to be very interesting. I could almost see how one might get tangled up in such a web of confusion.

Everyone looked as though they were having a good time. That was the problem—what kind of value would one place on a good time and to what extent would most people go?

As I looked around the room I could see people who hit all different sides of the spectrum. But regardless of what it was, it was definitely apparent to me that this was not the lifestyle for me. The smell of the liquor turned my stomach, and the smoke in the air just burned my eyes.

I was having a hard time—a very hard time—and then I began to wonder what anyone could expect to get out of this and moreover what did Ida expect. I was saddened by what I saw around me, so I got up and found my way to the door. I got back into the car and I began to drive some more but it seemed that now I was even worse off than before.

It was chilly outside and at times I could hardly see my way and then on top of that I began to cry. I kept thinking, what am I going to do? And so I decided to drive by the graveyard where Mama was buried. When I arrived I got out and went to the grave site. As I stood there I began to talk to Mama, I asked her over and over again what was I going to do. The rain began to pour down but I did not care as I fell to my knees and groveled for help. After a while I tried to compose myself as I walked cautiously to the car. I got in and closed the door and began to wipe the running water off my face then I headed for home.

On the way home I chose to take the scenic route. It was very dark and hazy out, when I was about two blocks from the house I saw the old church I had gone to from time to time. It sat far off the road up on a big hill. It was a white building but for some reason the church seemed larger than normal.

It seemed as if it were animated. Why? I do not know, because everything was so hazy, but there it was. As I rounded the next curve all I heard was a loud bang and that was the last thing I remembered.

And as I prepared to read the lines that followed, I sat up erect and read each word with much intent, because I never knew what had happened that night and I wanted to know more.

When I came to, a lot of people were standing over me. As I looked around I saw red and blue lights flashing, and I could hear people talking about what sounded like an accident. I tried to lift my head up to look around, to see more, but as I looked up all I could see in a distance was that church on the hill.

The paramedics put me into the ambulance and took me to the hospital. Little did I know then it would be weeks before I knew the full extent of what had happened. I was in the hospital what seemed like forever and it was particularly hard for me. I knew that this was the same place where my mother had lost her last battle with fate and that made me much more determined to win my war.

On about the fifteenth day the doctors came to me and told me that they would have to operate on my legs again. They said it would probably be a while before I was able to walk on my own. Because I had two fractured femurs. But aside from that they assured me that I would recover.

As the doctors gave me their prognosis I listened attentively as they talked. But despite their skepticism, I was determined that I would win no matter what the circumstance or the odds. They all said that it was a miracle that I was still alive but it wasn't enough for me. It wasn't until about two weeks later when I learned that I had been hit that night by a drunk driver.

I found it really ironic that my mom had been an alcoholic for most of her life and had lost her life to alcoholism and there I was fighting for my life as a result of another alcoholic. I became very angry because I felt as though it had cheated me. First it cheated me out of my mother and now I refused to let it have my life. I felt all of the emotions coming back. I tried to fight it but the harder I fought the more those old memories began to haunt me.

Having nothing but time on my hands I would just sit in the hospital room most of the day, except when I went to therapy. I was doing as well as could be expected I guess, but I still was not progressing the way I thought I should.

Sarah would come by and visit me from time to time but Ida never came. I wasn't surprised because she didn't even go and visit Mama when she was on her death bed. So why in the world would she bother to come and see me? Everyday that I lay in the hospital it was a constant fight not to have my spirit broken by anyone or anything. I was determined that I would win no matter what the doctors said. Lying there one evening I found myself dreaming about the accident.

It was a rainy night and darkness surrounded me. It was so compelling and then somewhere on the top of a hill nearby I saw an old white church. It seemed as if everything was magnified, as if someone had pressed rewind.

There I was rounding the corner again. I turned my head and I saw a church up on the hill. Then the whole picture just paused right in front of me. There stood that church as if it was in 3D.

I began to toss and turn and all of a sudden I heard someone call my name. It was the nurse who had come to give me my medicine. I took the medicine and then I laid back down to try and get back to sleep, but I couldn't.

Now it seemed as if this church was haunting me. What could it mean? And I began to dream once more. In the dream everything was tranquil, the grass was very green and kind of tall, but not too tall and nearby sat an old swing set. I guess it was there for the children.

The church sat a ways back off an old dirt road. As I walked a little closer up the dirt road, I could see the building more clearly. It was a plain little white wood building with a big cross over top of it. I walked up the steps and cautiously opened the door and peaked inside.

There I saw two aisles of pews. I cautiously looked around, tiptoeing down the aisle as the wooden floor boards creaked and crackled. At last I made it to the altar where ahead of me I saw a podium and the pulpit was directly in front of me.

I could see a stained glass window with all sorts of colors. In the picture was a man in a white robe with his hands held out. I stood and stared at the window in amazement, wanting to say something but unable to find the words. Soon I fell to my knees and began to ask, why? "What do you want from me?" "What does it all mean?" I just kept staring at that window, and then in the blink of an eye it was all gone and I was standing in an open field in the middle of nowhere. In an instant, I dashed to my feet and I began to look all around but there was nothing, there was no one to be found.

I then screamed and yelled but no one answered because no one heard. Then I heard a voice say, no one can hear you because you are all alone. I began to panic and I ran as hard and as far as I could but I still heard no one and I saw nothing.

Then I sat up in my hospital bed. As I began to analyze the dream it gave me an eerie feeling because this was the same dream I had been wrestling with for years. The people, the places, and the scenery was different but I was certain that the meaning was the same.

Before it was me and the ocean and now it was me in a field; it all came back to the same thing. I kept running and running although I couldn't figure out why, "what was I running from?" And if it frightens me that much I wondered did I really want to know.

I laid there most of the night thinking, just staring at the ceiling. When I looked over toward my window I noticed a new day was dawning right before my eyes. I scurried over toward the hospital window and sat in a nearby chair while I watched the sun come up over the horizon.

It had been such a long time since I had seen the sun rise and even longer since I had taken the time to enjoy it. As I sat there, I began to bath in its beauty, in its warmth.

I stood up and gazed into its eyes, as a feeling of serenity rose up inside of me. I began to think how astounding it was to watch a thing of such beauty and grace. After a while I decided to go back and lay down so I could try and catch up on some sleep. While in the process of making my way back to the bed, I stopped at my night stand and opened the drawer. There I found a bible laying inside. I paused for a moment and then I reached down and placed my hand on it.

I began to run my fingers across it as if I were reading Braille, but I was hesitant to pick it up. It took me back to when Mama was in the hospital and I use to read to her. I stepped back and closed the drawer because I was determined not to go back into the past. Yet I knew that it was the only way for me to truly heal all of the pain and get on with my life.

I stepped back toward the drawer and took a deep breath. As I opened it, I reached down inside, grabbed the little black book and set it down on the bed. I knew that at some point I would be forced to see the truth about myself, and my family. And the thought scared me because I did not know if I was ready to

handle the truth. *As I gazed at the book a little more, I opened it and the first page I turned to was the book of Genesis and it said;*
In the beginning God created the heaven and the earth
and the earth was without form and void. And darkness was
upon the face of the deep and the spirit of God moved upon
the face of the waters
and God said, "Let there be light,"
As I sat there I thought back to that beautiful sunrise and my mind could not began to perceive how someone could have created something so magnificent just by speaking it into existence.

As I went on reading I began to pick up where Mama and I left off. By that point I knew that this was where I would find my truth. In about the next six weeks I finished reading the Bible from cover to cover and it gave me a certain sense of peace and accomplishment; yet I still lacked the full understanding that went along with it.

That night I kneeled down to pray and I asked God for understanding. To tell you the truth, that was when everything started. I found a new sense of peace as well as a new life. Suddenly everything I had read started taking on a new meaning, and that began the first day of my new birth, my new beginning. It all started right there in that hospital room.

Nothing was there to distract me—nothing but me and I had already waged that war and lost. I now know that something good did come out of the accident.

As I stood there peering out of my hospital window, as the hot soothing sun shone brightly upon my face, I thought about the prayer I had prayed the night before. All of a sudden it was as if a light bulb went on inside my head.

Suddenly I began to see a much bigger picture. All I'd ever known about religion was that people got saved and they were supposed to go to church. But on that day I found out what it meant to be a Christian. It all started with a belief and as I began to think about it one particular word kept coming to mind—the word believe. I had just read the Bible from cover to cover and it was then more than ever I had to know more, I just had to. I then began to ask myself some leading questions.

First, I asked myself, did I believe that God created the world? As I looked out that window and up at the sky I saw the most beautiful array of clouds I believe I have ever seen. I unequivocally answered yes to the first question. I believe that something that magnificent had to have been created. I could not imagine all of it happening by some strange accident or the big bang theory which was what they taught us in school.

I then went on to assess the Bible as a whole. I felt I could not accept one part and then deny another part. My assumption was that the Bible as a whole had to be taken as a whole and not by books or parts, verses or chapters.

I realized that much like many other things in life, this too could not be separated. Right at that moment I began to say, "I believe God created this earth and everything on it." I then said;

"I also believe that Jesus is the son of God and that there is a heaven and a hell."

I think I must have stood there for several more minutes just saying it over and over again, "I believe." It was then that I began to feel a sudden tingling come over my body and it felt so very different and yet it felt good. As I stood there I began to bathe in the freshness of the Lords' sun.

About that time a nurse came in to carry me down to physical therapy. I was determined as usual, but even the therapist noticed that there was a certain meekness about me that day. The first thing she asked was, "are you feeling okay?" I told her yes, I felt fine. It meant the world to me for her to notice a change for the better.

I had to pause once again as I thought about my sister's trials. It seemed I was facing some of those very same dilemmas in my life. I could see that she had found a solution to her problem, but how I wondered if it work for me.

I was still determined to have a full recovery but now it was for different reasons. Before it was to avenge myself after Mamas' death as well as to wage an all—out war against drugs. But since I had been there I had learned better and that was no longer my intent. I just wanted to get well just for the sake of getting well. The next day the doctor came back into my room to give me the results on my follow-up. The prognosis was very good, he said; I had all but recovered and there was only a little stiffness left in my right leg.

He then went on to say that I could probably resume a normal life within the next couple of months. I was more than excited to get the news. I knew that at last I would be going home.

The next morning I woke up bright and early. I began to gather the few personal items I had accumulated while I was there. I then took a seat in the chair that sat cater corner to my bed. I sat there clenching my cane in one hand, as I waited for Sarah to pick me up.

I thought about the last couple of months I had spent in the hospital. I thought about the healing that had taken place, not only of my physical body but also of my mind. As I glanced around the room I saw the black Bible sitting on the night stand. And a smile came over my face as if I were saying that this was where it all started. I nodded my head in agreement and took a mental picture of the room.

How ironic it was! This place where so many sick people suffer and die had become a safe haven for me because I found a sanctuary within its walls. Sarah then walked in and asked me if I was ready to go.

She began to tell me about how things were going with Ida as she picked up my suitcase and she headed out of the door. I got up and hobbled behind her but at the doorway I turned back around for one last look. Softly I said to myself, "this was where it all began."

That was my way of validating everything that had happened in that room, a way of assuring myself that it was only the beginning because everything I had learned, I would use. I began to get teary-eyed because I really did not want to leave; I was afraid that I might lose everything I had just found.

Sarah was standing down at the end of the corridor. She told me that she had already taken care of the paperwork, she then helped me out to the car.

Chapter Eight

ՇՑ֍Ͻ

My Change Had Come

Finally I'd made it through yet another book. As I put the book down I looked to the table that sat beside my bed at the one book that remained and wondered just what lie within its pages. I knew that I was nearing the last couple of years of my sister's life.

Everything that I had read that day and all of the other days began to sink down inside of me. Once again morning came and I went about my daily chores. There was so much to do since I was only months away from the completion of my sentence. But when I found the time I continued reading.

On the way home I was very quiet. Sarah began telling me about the meal that she had prepare for me and soon after we came upon the place where I had my accident. We began to round the curve and as we did my heart began to beat hysterically. I yelled at Sarah to stop the car. She slowed down and then stopped along the side of the road. I sat there for a moment as I

*caught my breath and then I got out of the car. Sarah followed.
She began to asked me what was wrong.*

*I replied, "nothing" as my eyes carried me a little further
across the road and over a hill. I could see that white, little
church sitting there.*

*I asked Sarah to drive me up to that church. At first she tried
to argue with me by saying I needed to go home and get some
rest, because I had just gotten out of the hospital. But I insisted
that we go and after a little persuasion, we headed up the long
dirt road. My eyes grew wider and wider as we neared the
church. Finally the car stopped, I got out and I looked around for
a moment or two.*

*Then I began to walk toward the church. It was a slow walk
since I was using my cane but eventually I made it to the front
steps. Sarah grabbed hold of my arms as she helped me climb the
steps. I then noticed some beautiful violet flowers planted on each
side of the steps. By this time I had caught a cramp in my other
leg but I did not say anything because I didn't want Sarah to
know I was in pain. Finally we reached a double door and Sarah
knocked several times but no one answered.*

*She then twisted the door knob and the door opened so we
went inside. I was astounded by what I found. Everything was
identical to my dream—the pews, the colors, everything. I began
to hobble down the aisle and as I drew closer I noticed the big
bay window directly behind the altar.*

*I could see and feel the light that was shining through the
stained glass windows. It was so radiant! I moved closer towards*

the altar and then I came face to face with the man who was in my dreams. There he stood above the pulpit, in a white robe with his hands stretched out to me in an inviting way. Then Sarah called my name, "Vileen, what are you doing?"

"We're going to get into trouble because we weren't invited here," But I was, she just didn't know. As I looked at the window I put down my cane, laid down at the altar and began to weep.

My cries must have echoed throughout that old church. Then Sarah told me that we had to go. I could feel her trying to pull me up off the floor, but I refused to move, or rather, I could not move. Then I heard another voice, it was a man's voice and I heard him say, "Let her alone, don't touch her."

I wept there for the longest time. I couldn't stop crying no matter how hard I tried. At times I would all but stop and begin to compose myself, and then out of nowhere I would start again. In the midst of everything I felt a hand touch me on my shoulder. As I turned my head to look up and see who it was, there was a man standing over me.

I could not see his face nor could I see what he was wearing at all because the sun was shining so brightly from behind him, all I could see was a silhouette. I reached for my cane as I scurried to get up. The gentleman took me by one arm and helped me to my feet. He then sat me down in a nearby pew.

Hello, he said. My name is Pastor Austin. He then told me that he was the pastor of the church. "Dear child, what is your name?"

"Vileen Ford."

"So what brings you here on a day like today?" He asked.

I told him about the accident, and about the dream, I had while I was in the hospital. I then turned to the minister and asked him, "what does it all mean?" He put his arms around me as he began to cut a little smile and then he said; "Vileen, I'll tell you what it all means; God had decided to use you in his kingdom and he is beckoning for you to let him in."

He went on to tell me that God wants and has a special need for every living creature but he also gives us a choice. He told me to put away all of my rationalization and reasoning. "Don't try and figure God out." He said.

"Learn to accept him for who he is; because too many people don't. They evaluate everything with their mind and if it is not rational or cannot be reasoned out then they say it must not be real. Which is not necessarily the case. The very thought of God creating the universe is overwhelming for most people to perceive and therefore the whole point of reading a Bible is absurd to them."

He then said that the experience I had in the hospital was real and the reoccurring dreams confirmed that. "Don't let anybody put you down or try minimize your experience," he said. Then he asked me, "Vileen, do you believe in God?"

I looked up at his tall dark face and I said "yes," and then he asked me if I believed that God had sent his only begotten Son, Jesus, who died for our sins so that we may have eternal life. I said "yes," once again. Then tears began to swell in my eyes as he clenched my hand.

We then held hands as he began to pray. At the time I did not understand the full magnitude of what was going on. Still I knew that would be a day I would always remember. When we knelt at the altar and began to pray I could feel a tingling coming over me.

At that moment there was so much peace as if the world had been lifted off of my shoulders. After he finished praying he invited me back to the church on Sunday to be baptized. As I walked back through the church I could feel heat radiating through my body. When I made it to the double doors, the pastor helped me down the stairs. Sarah was waiting in the car. I got in and we drove off. I was so happy, I wanted to tell the world.

I started to tell Sarah but she shut me up real quick. It was as if she didn't want to hear a single word. She kept changing the subject and acting as if she didn't hear me. At first I was hurt but then I realized that I was expecting too much from her. The rest of the ride home was quiet—I don't believe a single word was spoken between us. It seemed as if she suddenly had an attitude toward me, but I couldn't figure out why. Instead I turned my thoughts to the tremendous experience I had just had.

At last we were home and I was exhausted. I went inside and ate a little something and before long I was fast asleep. I must have been sleeping for about three hours when I was awakened by some loud and crazy music Ida was playing. I got up and went to the front room and asked her if she could please tone the noise *down. I reminded her that I had just gotten out of the hospital. As usual she had something smart to say, but I refused to argue and fight with her, I was just too tired. Instead I went back to my room and closed the door. But the noise continued. I wanted to say something to her but I didn't. It would have only made things worse.*

That night seemed to last forever. Eventually somewhere in the wee hours of the morning all of the loud music stopped and I was able to get some rest. At last it was morning and I felt awful. It was the first night I'd slept in my bed in a long while. My body was sore and I felt groggy so I laid in bed until about mid-afternoon. When I got up I straightened up around the house and fixed myself a bite to eat. Then I sat in the front room and waited for Ida to get home. Eventually she came strolling in about eight-thirty that evening.

When she came through the door I told her that I wanted to talk to her. She tried to brush me off the same way she did everyone else; by telling me that she was right in the middle of something and that she would get back with me. My voice grew louder as I became more forceful with her. I wanted to let her know that we really needed to talk.

She then gave me permission to go ahead and talk as long as I hurried it up. I said, "Ida we have a problem," she just gazed at me with a disrespectful look on her face, and it angered me. In that moment I knew that things were going to be more difficult than I had ever expected.

"I want to share something with you," I said.

She still looked at me with a dumbfounded look on her face as if she was saying so what. However, I decided to go-ahead and tell her about my experience anyway. I figured if I told her perhaps it would evoke some kind of positive response. I couldn't have been more wrong instead she just looked at me with a blah reaction on her face as if she didn't care. Although it hurt me I tried hard not to let it show.

PS. Until tomorrow, I'm not the same anymore

Dear Diary,

Today is September 25, 1990. It has been several months since my discharge from the hospital and things are going well with me but Ida continues to lay heavy on my heart. Yesterday I had to have a talk with her about her behavior. "Ida," I said "things are going to have to change around here." I could tell by her facial expression that she was starting to get angry.

I knew that an all-out confrontation was at hand. Then she began to go off on a tangent saying all sorts of things. "Why should I have to change my whole life-style because you woke up one morning and decided that you were going to get saved?"

"Yes," I said. "I wish you could find what I had found," but—before I could finish my sentence she jumped in again and told me how she was grown and could do as she pleased. Then she said, "I don't need anyone telling me what they expected of me and whether I end up like Mama or not is my choice." I tried to explain to her that it was a lot more than that. I didn't want to

see her end up like Mama and I was worried about her health as well as her safety. There was nothing else for me to say so I just shut up. I think that was the first time I thought about giving up on her and moving out of the house.

All of my life I had looked out for Ida as a big sister should. But nothing I did or tried to do ever fazed her and now the time had come when I felt as if there was nothing more I could do for her. I slowly and calmly walked back to my room. At that time I hadn't fully made up my mind as to what I was going to do about moving out of the house. I figured that eventually Ida would turn herself around and that it wouldn't be too long.

I just nodded my head in agreement as I finished reading the accounts of the talk that we had. I remembered that day and I knew she was right. I felt as though Vileen was always trying to tell me what to do, trying to change me. Even worse, I already felt guilty about not being there for her or Mama, but at times I felt as though she would never let me forget it. At that time I was glad she was moving out, I thought that things would be better that way.

After I got to my room I started preparing myself for Sundays' service. As I did my spirit lifted and before I knew it found myself singing. The only thing on my mind was the baptism. After I finished getting my clothes ready, I sat down for a brief moment and read my Bible.

I read St.John the third chapter, about a man name Nicodemus who began to question Jesus about being born again. How could a man be born of water and of spirit, without which he could not enter into the kingdom of heaven?

That was very hard for Nicodemus to understand and like Nicodemus I found myself to be mislead or confused by the whole thing. At some point in my life, I'd heard about people getting baptized however; I always thought of it as a ritual. Besides I never really gave much thought to the meaning behind it. But as I sat there and pondered over the verse I could plainly see that the baptism was more than a ritual, that the water was significant in and of itself.

I was very excited about the day that followed so I wasted no time getting to sleep. With Ida gone the house was quiet and before I knew what had hit me, it was morning. I got up and called Sarah to remind her to pick me up and take me to church.

After I finished getting dressed, I went out and sat on the porch to wait for Sarah, but she never came. I went back inside to try and think of someone else I could call to pick me up and take me to church. I couldn't think of anyone else right off hand but then I remembered one of the ladies who had come to Mamas' funeral. She had given me her number and told me that if I ever needed anything to her give her a call.

So I rummaged through the house for her number. Because it had been about a year since I had talked with her, I was a little hesitant to call; I didn't think that she would remember me. But I went ahead and dialed the number anyway.

The phone rang about eight times before someone answered.

"Hello," she said.

"Hello Ms. Brown," I replied. "It's me Vileen Ford."

"Yes, honey what do you need?"

I asked her if she could pick me up on her way to church. Ms. Brown then told me that she was just on her way out of the door to go to church herself. "I'll be glad to pick you up," she said. She arrived at my house in about five minutes.

On the way to church, I briefly shared my life-changing experience with her. She seemed so happy. I could see the tears swelling up in her eyes. A feeling of joy and of unconditional acceptance came over me and soon we were at the church. We were about ten minutes late but it didn't matter to me. Because I was just so happy to be there. Mrs. Brown helped me up the stairs and into the church.

I will never forget that Sunday. It is as clear in my mind as if it were yesterday, although there are things that happened last week that I can't even recall. The message that Sunday was, "Have you had your bread today?"

"The bread I am speaking of can't be found in any grocery store," said Pastor Austin.

"I am talking about the bread of eternal life." He read from the book of John, and as I sat there and listened I was captivated by his sermon. Although the church was full that Sunday, it seemed as if he was talking directly to me.

I listened closely as he explained; he said the bread that he was speaking of was Jesus—he was the living bread and if any man eat of it he shall have everlasting life. He went on to clarify by reading St. John 6:51 "I am the living bread, which came down from heaven: if any man eat of this bread, he shall live forever: and the bread that I give is my flesh, which I will give for the life of the world."

The pastor said, "there are many of you who are hungry with a hunger that can not be satisfied. Nothing you do seems to make you happy. It isn't a physical hunger but rather a spiritual hunger and the only way that hunger can be quenched is spiritually."

He then said, "the Bible is our source of spiritual food. We feed our physical body everyday—in most cases three or more times a day—so why can't we also feed our spiritual bodies in the same manner."

At that very instant I felt as if a volt of electricity ran through my body. I began to look around to see if anyone else was having the same reaction to the sermon. Everyone looked comfortable, they were waving their hands, nodding their heads and saying an amen or two.

All of a sudden it was as if I was on fire and I began to twitch and turn; it seemed as if I just could not sit still. Then I heard the pastor say the doors of the church were open and if anybody would like to accept Jesus Christ as their personal Savior, they should please come forward.

I sat there glued to my seat afraid to move as the choir sang "I don't feel no ways tired." Something inside of me began edging me to accept the invitation I hesitated for a brief moment and then I stood up. It was as if everything went into slow motion and someone had turned the sound off. As I looked around me, I could still see people clapping and their mouths moving, but I heard nothing. I began to cross over people trying to get out into the aisle. Then slowly I walked down the aisle with the help of my cane. I could feel the sun beaming on me as it shone through the windows of the church.

It was a beautiful sight and thinking back I can hardly ever remember a day when the sun didn't light up that church. I never could figure out just how the sun reflected off of those windows to make such a beautiful collage of light. I think that like me everyone felt as though it was a sign or a gift from God, so we always cherished its beauty.

Finally I made it down to the alter. Pastor Austin embraced me and asked me if I wanted to accept Jesus Christ as my personal Savior. I replied "yes," and the whole congregation began to clap, while others cried. I was really overcome by it all as the choir sang another song.

The pastor told me to come back that afternoon so I could be baptized. After service Ms. Brown took me out to lunch and we talked about the baptism that was to follow in just a matter of hours. When we returned I walked back behind the church and I saw the lake I was supposed to be baptized in.

A couple of shade trees stood off to the side and a gentle breeze was blowing, it was a beautiful sun-shining day, I couldn't think of a better day for a baptism. Soon it was time for me to get changed into my clothes for the baptism. Everyone had gathered around the lake and there I stood in a white gown.

Then I saw pastor Austin walking out into the lake. I followed, although I was terrified! Because I knew I didn't have full balance in my legs. Yet slowly I journeyed out into the water after him and when I reached him, he grasped my right hand with his right hand.

As I stood cater corner to him he placed his left hand behind my back, to give me support and then he asked me did I believe that God sent his Son Jesus who died on Calvary, so that all men might be free. I replied "yes," and then he asked me if I would like to accept Jesus Christ into my life, to be my personal Savior. I said "yes," once more.

He then put his right hand over my face as he said, "by the profession of your faith, I now baptize you in the name of the Father, the Son and the Holy Ghost," he then proceeded to dunk me under the water. Everything happened so quickly, yet when I think back on it, the moment seems to last forever.

I left there that day feeling refreshed and renewed. But when I got home there was an all-out battle raging. The question still remained, what was I going to do with Ida. I knew that the best thing I could do for her would probably be for me to move out of the house. I felt as if I'd done everything I could do and it was time for her to be more responsible for herself.

I made up my mind that evening that I would pray about it to see if I felt the same way the next day. Soon morning came seeping over the old building across the street as it had so many times before until it had become all too familiar to me. Still its beauty always had a way of entrancing me. The day had finally come and I knew just what I needed to do. I only woke up determined to see some changes and fast. All I had to do now was to find a way to tell Ida. I decided to spend the day looking for a new apartment. I went down to the local corner store; got a newspaper and began to read the classifieds. There were only two places that interested me.

I wanted to go ahead and get a place that way I wouldn't be able to change my mind. So I went to look at two apartments neither of which were that great. However I finally decided to take the second one, located on Jasper street two blocks from the local community college. By the time I got back home I was exhausted but I knew that I had a lot of packing to do.

Then about nine o'clock Ida came home with a couple of her friends. I met them at the door and politely told them there wasn't going to be a party tonight because Ida and I were going to have a talk. She resisted and beckoned them to come on in, but I gave them a stern look and one of the guys said "perhaps another night would be better," and they left. Ida then began to go off on one of her tantrums.

But somewhere In the middle of it all, I do not know where it came from but it was as if something just rose up inside of me and said no, not this time. Then I said, "Ida enough is enough and I have had it with your tantrums, your bad attitude and your loud parties. I have tried to talk to you about it civilly and all it has gotten me is more abuse. I have bent over backwards trying to help you in anyway I can looking after you, and taking care of you."

I then turned to her and said; "Ida, you are not a baby anymore and according to you, you don't need a friend, or a sister. You don't need anybody because you have everything under control." I then told her that I knew I was trying to be more than just a sister to her, because of the loss of our Mother.

"Well, nobody asked you to do anything for me," she replied.

"I know"—and then the tears began to swell up in my eyes.

"As I told her that I did things for her because I wanted to. I said, the only mistake I made was; I thought that you wanted my help. But from this day forward you are going to be on your own."

It took a moment for me to muster up just enough strength to say; "Ida I'm moving out!" I told her that it was because she decided a long time ago that she did not need me, Mama or anybody else, and with that I went to my room and I began to pack my things.

Thinking back, I'm sure Ida thought my leaving home was the best thing that could have happened to her at the time. But I am certain that now it is a day that time will never let either of us forget. Although we've never enjoyed the bond that most sisters share, that moment changed our relationship forever.

Meanwhile I packed all through the night. I was here, there and all through the house. Then Ida came to me and told me that there were certain things I could not take out of the house. I didn't try to argue with her.

Instead I just went on packing around her. It took me about two days to get all of my things moved from the house to the new apartment. After I'd finished moving, I went back to say good-bye to my neighbors.

PS. Until tomorrow, as my broken heart mends

Chapter Nine

⚭

Learning To Lean

As I sat there I began to think about the day that my sister moved out of the house and I remembered not wanting her to leave. I also remembered not having the courage to ask her to stay. After all, I had put her through so much.

Dear Diary,

Today is March 3, 1991. The first couple of days in the new apartment were though—real tough. It was so peaceful and quiet at night until I would lay awake and listen to the refrigerator that would come on from time to time.

It was most definitely an adjustment but it was welcomed and long overdue. Soon the months began to pass. I was still going to the church down the street from house. Sometimes after church I would stop by to see Ida but she was hardly ever home. When she was she always had a house full of company. So I usually didn't stay long. It really depressed me to see how she was just letting herself go down.

The last time I saw her it looked like she had lost quite a bit of weight. She was looking pretty bad and that worries me. But no matter how often I visit and try to help her, there is only so much she allows me to do. There are times when I question my decision. I wonder just what I have gained by moving out because most of my days and nights are spent worrying about Ida.

Dear Diary,

Today is August 4, 1991. Over the next year or so it was the same old, same old. There were too many ups and downs to recall but it was always the same basic scenario. She would call me to come over and talk. Then when I got there she would tell me about how she planned to make this great big turn-around in her life, that she had finally taken a good look at her life and she didn't like what she saw; and of course, she vowed to change.

She would then apologize to me and ask for my support. And as always I was in agreement with her, hoping that each time would be her last time. But that day as of yet has not come. Ida is beginning to use more dangerous drugs and it is beginning to lead her into escapades with the police.

My only sister is heading down a dead-end path and there is nothing I can do to stop her. Meanwhile I am going on with my life. I've started going to the community college just around the corner and I'm taking business classes at night, at the Old

Caldwell Building. One night I was walking across the campus and I saw a face that looked familiar. Then I noticed that he was looking at me, as if he might have known me also, but he was just too scared to approach me.

The next day I saw him again but this time I found the courage to approach him. When I got close enough I called out, "Stanley," and to my surprise he turned around and said, "Vileen." "Yes," I replied. We then proceeded to give each other a big hug. That night we had dinner together as we talked about how he ended up moving to Kentucky.

I was so surprised to see him; he was the same old cheerful person he had always been. However he did seem to be much more mature. He was not the same tall scrawny fellow he use to be. Now he is a rather attractive man although he has put on some weight but it looks good on him.

It was amazing to see how a couple of years had changed him. We spent the next couple of weeks, I guess you could say romancing each other. It was soon clear that we were very much in love.

PS. Until tomorrow, the future looks a lot brighter

Dear Diary,

Today is February 1, 1992. Stanley and I got married about six months ago. To tell you the truth, last year came and went so fast until I hardly even noticed it. Because I was so into Stanley and it was as if nothing else existed. We've been married several months now and we have had our ups and downs, our trials and tribulations. But somehow we've always managed to make it through the hard times.

It was about a month ago when Stanley came home and told me he had been laid off his job, due to a major downsizing of the company. Everything started to go down hill from there. All of a sudden it was as if he had become someone I did not know. And as the weeks passed It only got worse. All of the extra stress was beginning to take a toll on me. I started working a second job to help out with the bills, but it still was barely enough to help us get by. And then about week later I found out that I was pregnant.

In a way I was happy but I knew that I had the awful task of going home and facing Stanley. I knew that somehow, someway I had to face him. When I got home that afternoon I waited until I got up the nerves to say; "Stanley, I'm pregnant." I could tell by the look on his face that he wasn't too happy. We both knew that the timing was wrong, but we also knew that the life growing inside of me was a sheer gift from God.

After we got over the initial shock we realized that there were so many things in our lives that were out of order. We wondered how in the world could we fix them in time for our new arrival. That is when Stanley and I decided that we had done all we could do and so we then put it in the hands of the Lord. Because we realized that without him we could never be the parents that God truly intended for us to be. I started to praying like I use to pray and we started going back to church. Soon I began to see that things were getting a little better. Stanley found a job and that made everything else around the house run a lot smoother.

———

Dear Diary,

Today is May 10, 1992. I feel as though I have found a new course, a new fight. My faith has been renewed and I am reading the Bible once again with such vigor. The more I read, the more I learn and the closer I feel to God. I now see myself as more than just a Sunday Christian, I want to practice my religion on a daily basis.

My faith has become more than a biblical thing, it has a lot to do with the Spirit also. Yesterday I read; St. John 4:23,24 where it says that the hour cometh and now is when the true worshippers shall worship the Father in spirit and in truth for the Father seeketh such to worship him. God is a spirit and they that worship him must worship him in spirit and in truth.

As I went on reading and studying I came upon St. John 14:16,17 which read; I will pray the Father and he shall give you another Comforter that he may abide with you forever, even the Spirit of truth whom the world cannot receive because it seeth him not, neither knoweth him, but ye know him for he dwelleth with you and shall be in you.

The more I read; the more I began to understand that the Holy Spirit was not someone whom I had the opportunity of just meeting at church on Sunday. He wants to dwell in my life everyday.

  PS. Until tomorrow, as I continue to press toward the mark

Dear Dairy,

  Today is March 17, 1993. On October 22, 1992, God blessed me with a beautiful daughter whom I named Naomi. Stanley has accepted Christ and everything was going well in our house with the new baby. Then one day I was driving home from the store and I saw that the old pool hall on the corner of Jasper street had burned down. For some reason I felt compelled to stop, so I did.

  That place held so many bad memories for me because in times past people were always hanging out there drinking and doing drugs. However, on that day I saw a man in the parking lot cleaning up some wreckage and so I decided to get out and talk with him. He soon began to express his excitement, not because the place had burned down but rather because the pool hall would no longer be there to pollute the neighborhood.

  The man, Mr. Paine said that the owners' were not insured so he didn't know what was going to happen to the property. We both knew that the alcoholics and the drug dealers would just find somewhere else to hang out. Then the man turned to me and said, "at least they won't be here in our face where we are forced to look at them everyday."

  I then replied in anger, that "yes that is fortunate for you but I have a sister who has been on drugs and alcohol for the last five years. Eliminating this building may signify some great accomplishment for you but for me out of sight is not out of mind. For me drug addiction and alcoholism is not somebody else's problem. Rather it is something that I live with each and everyday."

About two weeks later Mr. Paine called me and apologized. He also told me that they were going to rebuild the building and try and turn it into a detox center. I thought that was a start; it was better than a pool hall. I discussed the idea with Stanley and we agreed to do all that we could to help get the project on its feet.

We called up the local church members and had them to pray as we were believing that everything would work out. There were many meetings between Mr. Paine and the other partners who had decided to join in to make it a neighborhood effort. At times it seemed as though we had underestimated the magnitude of the project.

We might have felt like we were in over our heads but the Holy Spirit was always there to comfort us and let us know that regardless of the obstacles we continually faced that God was on our side and that let us know that somehow everything would be all right.

As the days passed one by one people began to drop out of the project for various reasons. This made the load that the rest of us had to carry much heavier and almost impossible at times but we knew that this was something that we had to do for the neighborhood.

We knew that it was something that would bring a lot of good. I believe that is what held the rest of us together until the building was finished—that and the sheer grace of God. After we got the building completed we started to feel a little bit more at ease because we knew that we were more than half way home.

After I finished working around the building one afternoon I decided to stop by and see how Ida was doing. Regrettably I must say that I was not surprised to find her very thin and her hair looked like it had not been combed in a week. When I walked in the door I got sick to my stomach because the house was such a mess.

And on that particular day she had an attitude. The moment I got in the door the first thing I heard was I don't know why you are wasting your time at that rehabilitation center. She said, "if people wanted to get off drugs and alcohol they can. Besides I have several friends who have been in and out of those kind of facilities and they said it was a big joke."

As usual she knew just what to say to get me angry. I then told her how I felt about the center. I said "Ida, there is nothing wrong with the program, but the problem arises when people like yourself abuse the program because they think that they are getting over. When in reality the only thing they are doing is setting themselves up to fail again."

I then said, "you also have a caring problem, you don't care about anybody including yourself because if someone truly wants help and is committed to make the changes needed, a rehabilitation program could be one of the best things to ever happened to them." Thinking back on it, I know I might have said a little too much, or maybe there could have been another way of saying what I said. But before I knew it, it was already out of my mouth and it was too late.

So I got in the car and left. I knew the manner in which I had spoken was wrong but I also knew that it was too late to take it back so I just asked the Lord to forgive me and I let it go. Instead I began to think along a more pleasant path because tomorrow was to be Naomi's first birthday.

The party was a blast—it was small but Naomi had the time of her life. As I watched her sit and play with the other children I felt so blessed to have such a precious gift in my life. I often wonder just what kind of influence Stanley and I are making in her life? What kind of person will she be? And what will she contribute to the world? I only hope and pray that the Lord will bless me to be around to see her grow up and come into her own.

About 6:30PM we started winding everything up because Stanley and I had a long day ahead of us now that the detox building was complete. Papers had to be signed and staff had to be hired. There was so much to do, we spent the next couple of months getting fully operational. Everyday was a challenge. Between employee problems, the patients and the people in our old neighborhood, we had our hands full.

One morning when I came into work someone had spray painted one side of the building. We had to scrape up the money to get the building repainted. We had one problem after another.

Everything from employee tardiness to theft. Without a doubt we had our hands full.

Dear Diary,

Today is December 12, 1994. We are about nine months into the program and everything is going according to plan, but we have noticed a problem with our recidivism rate. Although by law we are well within what is required, it just isn't good enough for me.

I know that there is more I can do. I desperately want every person who walks out of the program to be a success, not just for a day or a week or even a month, but for a lifetime. I know within my heart that all of this is possible. Stanley and I have talked about it from time to time.

I suggested that we somehow integrate religion into the program. It only makes sense to me. Before I was only concerned about saving every Ida I met, I guess because I felt that in some way it might compensate for me not being able to reach her.

Now I have an opportunity not only for me to help someone get off of drugs or alcohol. But I also see this as an opportunity to show them the way to eternal life. It makes perfect sense to me but of course there are legal ramifications. Still, I feel in my heart it is the only thing to do.

Dear Diary,

Today is December 30, 1994. Yesterday is gone and it is a new and glorious day and with it we have found ourselves in the mist of a horrendous battle. Because the county agrees that there is a drug and alcohol problem and it only makes sense to have a rehabilitation center, they said. However, when religion got into the picture, all of a sudden it was a completely different story.

A committee said that we weren't allowed to force our religious belief on our patients; if we did that would change the whole purpose of the mission at hand. But I was determined that no matter what they said, there was a higher authority.

I spent the next couple of days on my knees in prayer and I can honestly say that God always comes through. I have learned through many ups and downs that God has been faithful to me even at times when I was so undeserving. Still it puzzles me, of all the things I've asked God to do he has done them in a nick of time, yet it seems as though my prayers for my sister Ida go unanswered.

After Stanley and I went to lawyers office for about the tenth time, they finally worked it out where we could integrate religion into our program. But they warned us that our admissions would go down because people wouldn't want to be hassled by religion.

I didn't care what they said because I knew that God had given me the go-ahead to do it, or rather he had put it in my spirit. I know that as long as I had his stamp of approval I didn't need anyone else's. I was going to go through with this regardless of what the staff said behind my back or what anyone else said; I had to.

PS. Until tomorrow, as I continue to press toward the mark

Dear Diary,

Today is March 12, 1995. The last couple of months Stanley and I have begun to see life in a whole different light. We now feel as though were making some headway and it really gives us a sense of accomplishment.

As I sit here today and look at where God has brought us from, I just can't believe it. We are getting ready to buy a house and it looks like the American dream that we always talked about will finally be ours. Right at this moment I wish that I could just stay suspended in time.

Everything is so perfect! Somehow, somewhere I have found an inner peace, an inner strength that surpasses all understanding and I know that this kind of tranquillity could only be a gift from God. Naomi is about three years old and she seems so impressionable.

As I sit here and watch her as she laughs and plays, I often think back on those years when I was her age and how I missed out on the very things that my daughter so joyously takes for granted. Sometimes it brings tears to my eyes as I replay those years through the innermost corners of my mind, and at times I find Naomi looking at me as she ask, "Mama, what's wrong?"

"Nothing," I say as I look down at her and give her a smile to reassure her that everything is all right.

I often find myself telling her little things, always hoping and praying that something will stick with her as she grows older. These are the best of times for her and I pray that they will never end.

      PS. Until tomorrow, as God continually keeps my child

Dear Diary,

Today is March 28, 1995. This morning when I awoke the phone was ringing. I started not to answer it however I ended up answering it anyway. It was Robert one of Ida's friends. My first thought was how did he get my number? And why in the world was he calling me? Then it dawned on me to ask if Ida was all right. He then told me that she was at Saint Joseph's hospital. I immediately dropped everything I was doing and left for the hospital.

I must admit that I was not ready to face what I found there in that hospital room. As the nurse showed me into her room I noticed a pale young girl weighing maybe eighty to ninety pounds lying in the hospital bed. As I walked closer I began to look harder but it wasn't until I got right over top of her and looked down into her pale, shriveled face I could see that she did bear a certain resemblance to my sister.

There was still a part of me that wanted, so much to deny that the person in the bed could be my sister. The nurse asked me if I was okay, I said "yes," as she showed herself out of the room. Slowly all of the energy I had began to be sucked out of me and my body went limp as all of the emotions began to overwhelm me. I saw a chair nearby so I grabbed it all at once in order for it to break my fall. And I just sat there and watched as a machine basically breathed for her.

There I sat trying to convince myself that she hadn't won, even though she had fought me relentlessly. No matter what I had tried to do, nothing ever seemed to get through to her. I thought that perhaps she had gotten what she wanted and for once she had won even if it was at the expense of her life. It only made me wonder what she might be thinking. Was she gloating in her victory and laughing at my defeat?

Then again, I thought perhaps she was finding that there is something more to life besides having a good time. Just maybe she was seeing that there was something after death. Then another thought crossed my mind. Could she be saying, "Vileen was right after all, and if I had it to do all over again I would listen to her."

I can't help but believe that Ida wants to find her way out but like too many others she is afraid to try because she feels unworthy. I also know that my whole attitude must change in order for me to help her. But she is going to have to meet me halfway and that is going to be the hard part.

I stood up by her bedside once again and as I took her hand and put it in mine. I said, "Ida, it's Vileen, if you can hear me I want you to know that I am here for you; I love you and God loves you no matter what."

I stayed by her bedside for about another hour and then I went home. By the time I got there everyone was asleep and I was glad because this gave me some time to go to the Lord in prayer. But before I got started I took a nice hot shower. Afterwards I went to the living room and sat down with my Bible.

I read several chapters and then I prayed and asked God to heal my sister—for him to give her a new mind and a new spirit. I was determined to receive a miracle. I went to bed that night feeling a lot better because I knew that I had prayed about it and I had left it in the hands of the Lord.

―――――――

Dear Diary,

Today is June 15,1995. The next morning when I got to the hospital the nurses were taking her temperature. As I got a little closer I could see that her eyes were open and she was no longer in a coma. I knew that there was a miracle in progress. And as the days passed we began to go through temper tantrums; phases where she didn't want me in her room, physical violence—it was hard. But knowing that Ida was just acting out because that was her way of trying to maintain some kind of control over her situation made it a little easier to take.

As the weeks began to pass, little by little it became apparent to her that regardless of what she was accustomed to, she couldn't do anything for herself. But now since she had to depend on someone for everything, for her very existence, I think it became apparent even to her that her attitude had to change and drastically.

Little by little I could see a new person emerging, one I hadn't known since Ida was a mere child. It felt good—very good, to finally see more than a familiar face but rather to see the sister I once had known. Ida was finally clean and I knew that this was her opportunity for a second chance at life if only she wouldn't screw it up.

PS. Until tomorrow, while I wait for a miracle

Chapter Ten

ﾃ3ﾃﾆ)

Finally I'm Free

I paused for a moment to reflect back on the time when I was in the hospital. I remember that being one of the most troublesome times ever, for the first time in a long while I was clean and sober and it scared me to death. But I continued to read;

Dear Diary,

Today is July 20, 1995. In the weeks that followed, in the evenings I would go and visit Ida at the hospital. One day I bought her a Bible and then all the way over to the hospital I worried about how I was going to present it to her. When I got there she had just finished with physical therapy and one of the nurses was pushing her back to her room in her wheelchair.

I walked along beside her as we talked. Finally the opportunity arose for me to tell her that I had a present for her. I could see the surprise and anticipation on her face. I then slowly handed her the Bible and to my surprise she did not say one single word. That was when I began to see that there had been more than a mere physical change. A long awaited miracle was unfolding right before my eyes. Although I must say that she didn't jump up and leap for joy, she did not reject it either and that was truly a great step.

In the evenings when I would go and visit her I would read the Bible to her. It wasn't easy. She challenged me on everything I said, sometimes before I could ever get it out of my mouth. I guess she was just asking all of the questions I once asked. She asked everything from; is there really a heaven or a hell, to if God is a loving God then how can he condemn us to hell? And on—and on she went.

I looked at her in amazement as she talked. She must have asked a dozen questions. I could see that the time had come for her to stop and think about what I'd been saying. I believe that it was starting to make sense to her. When I left the hospital that night I knew that somehow, some way everything would be all right. It was just a matter of time.

Meanwhile the program was still coming along. Our attendance had gone down quite a bit but I was convinced that it would start picking back up eventually. After all, what Stanley and I are doing is not for our own gratification but I feel that it is for the glorification of God.

Not only are we helping people get cleaned up but we are also giving them something that will change their lives forever. I once heard a preacher say when you have come in contact with God, no matter who you are, your life will never be the same.

That phrase always echoes throughout the walls of my heart because I know that I've been giving my patients more than just therapy. I am exposing them to the source of all knowledge and power.

PS. Until tomorrow, troubles don't last always

Dear Diary,

Today is August 1, 1995. I went to church yesterday and it was a miraculous service. Many souls were saved and as a result I felt so much joy on the inside. But I couldn't help but think about my sister in the hospital and how wonderful it would be to see her come to Christ. The thought just brought tears to my eyes; as I sat there in the pews I began to cry. Stanley leaned over and asked, "what's wrong?" "Nothing" I said, "just thinking about Ida." He understood; thinking about Ida always made my heartache.

Since I have been saved it is as if I hardly ever have time to concentrated on me. Instead I often find myself thinking back to the person I used to be and the way my life was and it always brings a smile to my face.

It reassures me of how awesome God really is. And everything I have experienced as a result of my profession of faith I want to share with someone else. That is what I have built my life around. A lot of days I wonder where would I be if Mama had not died in that hospital room; if there hadn't been a Bible there for me to read. Perhaps I would be like my sister, Ida, strung out on drugs or even worse. I am sure that whatever life I would have been living, it wouldn't be as fulfilling or as gratifying as this one.

After service we went home and had a nice big Sunday dinner. It reminded me of how I always wished things could have been around our house many years ago. But that no longer matters because now I know exactly what kind of life I want for Naomi, and I know if I set a good example for her and give her a strong nurturing home environment, she will have a better chance at getting it right the first time around.

Perhaps so many precious years of her life won't have to be wasted searching for something. She might not ever have to know the emptiness that so many people experience. That is why everyday is a challenge for me to strive for excellence. I know that every step I take I bring not only myself but also my daughter that much closer to our journeys end.

That is why I take full responsibility for defining the boundaries for her because I know if I lay down the standards she may follow. Besides I feel as though God has given me this virtuous task of watching and praying for her.

Dear Diary,

Today is September 2, 1995. The next day brought with it another sigh of well-deserved relief. Work went well and we got another contract that Stanley and I had been praying for.

Everything finally seemed to be falling into place. Although I knew that someday there would be another test, perhaps another trial. But I also knew that with the help of the good Lord he would see us through them all.

That afternoon I stopped by the hospital as usual and Ida was looking good, very good. I could see that for the first time in a long while, when she looked in the mirror, she really liked what she saw.

I asked her had she started reading the Bible I had given her and she hesitantly said "yes, I've read a couple of verses here and there." And that was all she said. I wondered, did she really get it, but I knew that I couldn't push it because I had made too much progress, so I just let it go.

Instead I took the opportunity to invite her to church with me when she got out of the hospital. I told her that I was not taking no for an answer. She just laughed and said okay. That night I practically ran home, I just couldn't wait to tell Stanley because we had been praying for her. That night was most definitely a time of jubilation around our house. But still, no matter how many battles we were winning it was apparent that the war was not yet won.

Yesterday I went down to the daycare where Naomi stays during the day. It seemed that one of the other children bit her. The daycare manager told me that if they caught the child they would discipline them but otherwise I had to understand that it was a public daycare. She went on to tell me that I couldn't expect my child to come to daycare and to leave unscathed. However, that was unacceptable to me because I felt as if more could or should be done.

But this just let me know that there are still battles to be fought and won—there are so many different fights. Until sometimes I just want to fight them all. But I know that I can only do what the Lord allows me to do. So in the meantime I've decided that the best thing I can do is to fight the good fight of faith.

Many things in this world trouble me but I know that someday, some way, somehow the walls will come tumbling down and all of the double standards and the rules that bind God's people will all break down. Someday rulers of great nations will bow down and profess to God almighty, that Jesus Christ is Lord. I know that day will come.

PS. Until tomorrow, when the lion shall lay down with the lamb

---

Dear Diary,

Today is September 25, 1995. Saturday was the big day that Ida was supposed to be released from the hospital. It marked a milestone in all of our lives. It had been a six-month recovery period for her, although there was still much therapy to be done; she was pretty much back to normal. I went to the hospital early to organize a farewell party for her. Stanley and Naomi came later. It was a wonderful day. Emotions were overflowing, and I felt for the first time in a long while I had my sister back.

I remember the short speech that she gave right after she cut the cake. Although Ida was never good at expressing herself, what she said that day meant the world to me. She said, "I'd like to thank everyone who worked with me during this tough period of my life. But I would especially like to thank my sister, Vileen, for being there for me even though I almost never have been there for her."

I will always cherish those words for I know that they came from the bottom of her heart. No matter how she might feel about me some days, I know that somewhere buried deep down in her is a heart full of love. I only hoped that all of the time we spent in the hospital getting to know each other once again was not wasted. Maybe at some point in the future we will be able to pick up where we left off and gradually move on with our lives.

After the party we agreed that Ida would come home and stay with Stanley and me for a couple of weeks until she felt comfortable. Well, the first week that Ida was here it went okay, I guess, but I started getting the feeling that perhaps it was just too much for her.

By the second week I could see her whole personality beginning to change and I was afraid that she would start hanging out with her old friends again, so I reminded her that she had promised to go to church with me on Sunday.

We all got dressed and we went to church, it was a wonderful service. When the Pastor opened the doors of the church, I wanted so badly for Ida to go up there. But she didn't and I was saddened by this because I felt as though this was my last chance.

I had gotten her as far as I could but now I could see that she was slipping back into her old ways.

The ride home in the car was very quiet; no one said a word. I just kept thinking how I am going to get her to church next Sunday. When I got home and went to my bedroom, I began to cry. A few minutes later Stanley came in and asked me why was I crying, I told him. He said something to me that made the most sense. He said, "Vileen you have bought Ida a Bible, you take every opportunity to try and witness to her, you've taken her to the church-there's nothing else you can do. Ida is going to have to do something for herself. She is going to have to have a desire to want to change; but she knows that no matter what she does or gets into, you are going to be there to help bail her out."

"You've always been there and she figures that you always will be. She is going to have to realize that no matter how much you love and pray for her you can't save her."

In that moment I realized that Stanley was only saying what I had been feeling for a long time. Still I just couldn't bring myself to take that attitude. I knew I had spent many nights worrying about her and I knew that some way it all had to end and perhaps I would have to back off a little bit because all of the love and concern were only making matters worse.

Dear Dairy,

Today is November 22, 1995. The next week didn't seem to go any better around the house. Ida was starting to get irritable. I suggested that perhaps she might like to go to work with me the next day. The next morning when we got to the detox center I showed her around and introduced her to the staff.

I could see that perhaps that wasn't such a great idea after all because slowly but surely she began to critique the program and its staff. I told her that perhaps if she wanted to work there she could take some courses at the local college and Stanley and I would help her out. But I could tell by the expression on her face that the idea was not a good one.

As usual Ida wanted what she wanted when she wanted it. What I had planned on being a day of restoration and sharing for both of us really turned out to be a long hard grueling day for me and her alike. As the weeks began to pass she gained more confidence and boldness. And as a result I could feel the distance growing between us.

At this point I don't know whether she knew it or even cared but this would be the last trip for me. There really would be no more. That is what I felt in my spirit and the thought really saddens me. I knew that somehow I had to find consolation and in turn I would find my strength.

That next week when we came home from work, we found that Ida had company. It was one of her old friends. I had known for sometime that everything was leading up to an all out show down. Stanley and I sat down and had a talk. We both decided that it was time for Ida to return home.

When we confronted her, she exploded on one of her tantrums. And suddenly we had become some of the worst people that God had ever put on the face of the earth. I let her know that she could still work at the center.

She adamantly replied, "I don't want or need anything else from you." I guess that was the day that I lost my sister forever. When she walked out of the door I felt that perhaps in time she would come to understand, but as the months began to pass that was the last time that I saw her or ever spoke to her.

PS. Until tomorrow, until my broken heart mends

―――――――――

Dear Dairy,

Today is December 12, 1996. It has been one year since I have seen my sister. I know that wherever Ida is, she still loves me in her own way. Therefore I feel that it is just a matter of time before our paths cross again. But as for me, I will continue to carry on the best way I know how. Besides there is no time for mourning nor is there time for tears.

Instead I drown myself in my work and my family. I am bound to make us a success although I know that at times I push them entirely too hard. I think that ultimately I force them to absorb some of my pain. Stanley and I are still working on the perfect marriage, if there is any such thing.

I still have my flaws; as he still has his. I think that ultimately we can come to a point where we are both comfortable with one another and in that I find a certain sense of pride. Naomi is growing so big and tall—she is hardly the scrawny little tot she

I can see that she is very comfortable with her environment and who she is and that lets me know that perhaps Stanley and I are doing something right. She's doing very well in school and she's getting old enough now where I think she is beginning to understand more about her role not only in the family but also in the world. And as for my relationship with my sister, I will just continue to live life from day to day, as I supposed she does.

Even though sometimes I wonder how Ida is, I always know that in her own way she is doing just fine. Everything else in my life is going extraordinary. We are planning a fund raiser in about two weeks from Saturday. I am so excited! I must say that we both are really looking forward to it.

PS. Until tomorrow, better days ahead

Those were the last words that my sister ever wrote. Emotions began to overwhelm me as I closed the little blue book. For many years I thought that I knew my sister but now I find out that I really didn't. It's only now that I find out how much she really loved me and it hurts—it hurts me to death.

Those diaries are the only real thing of value that my sister left me because all of the other things mean absolutely nothing to me. But within those little blue books I will always have her memories, what meant the most to her while she lived.

I must say that reading those books the last couple of months while I was in prison really changed my life. Because I do not intend to let her death be in vain. Many times I stop and wonder why so many lives had to be lost just so mine might be saved. Perhaps If I would have straightened up sooner, Mama and Vileen might still be alive today. But I guess that is just something I will always wonder about.

The mailman just sighed as he shook his head and said, "wow! to look at you I would have never known you'd had such a troublesome life. So how did you find the strength to get to where you are today?"

The whole ordeal was a horrible experience for me because for the first time in a very long time I had to stop and think about someone other than myself and it really scared me. I had a niece whom I dearly loved who didn't have a family, and I had some social worker telling me how I would hardly be a fit guardian for her.

I knew that I had to find a way to get my life together for Naomi's sake. As I sat there in that prison day after day, I kept going over the events that happened the day of the accident, replaying the tape over and over again in my head. Then one day when I was standing in my favorite spot looking out of the window, I was distracted for some reason.

Turning to go back to my cot, I noticed a black Bible on the table by my bed. I never really noticed it lying there; it was as if it were just a fixture before that day. As I walked over to the table I reached down to pick the book up. But I hesitated—I guess a certain sense of fear came over me. But I knew that I had to have a change in my life.

Vileen had always talked so much about the Bible and God. Perhaps that was the way, I thought. So I reached down and picked the Bible up off the tiny table and went and sat down on my cot. I must have sat there for at least an hour with the Bible there before me. I just sat and stared at the book. All of the things that my sister and everyone else had ever told me about the Bible and religion began to rush through my mind.

As I began to open the Bible I thought about how I didn't have anyone who could teach me. However, I knew how desperate I was to have the kind of life that my sister had. But most of all I wanted another chance to start over.

But I just felt so unclean, so unworthy. I had spent a lifetime raising hell, cursing, smoking, partying. Not only did I curse and mock God but I did everything and anything I wanted to do. Yet there I sat wanting and hoping for another chance. I wanted it more than anything so before I opened the Bible I said a prayer.

I remember the words so plainly and so clearly because they were just so simple. I just told him, "Lord, I know that I haven't been a angel. I've been far from that and Lord, I feel as though I am not worthy of you, but Lord if you would just take me and give me a new life like you gave my sister, I promise from this day forward that I will serve you for the rest of my days."

Then I slowly opened the Bible and turned to St. John. I began to read chapter eight. The words just jumped off of the page at me. Verse seven read, "He that is without sin among you, let him first cast a stone at her." The story really moved me because here was this woman who was an adulteress. The world was ready to stone her to death because of her sin, but Jesus protected her and then he convicted those who condemned her.

As I read on through the chapter I began to feel my burdens become a little bit lighter. Before I had opened that Bible I felt so unworthy of God's love, of his forgiveness because the world had always judged me and I was tried, convicted and sentenced to a career of a lifelong failure, and a drug addict. And just as sure as the world found me hopeless and unworthy, I began to see myself in much the same manner.

Now contrary to what the world said, I found within the pages of the Bible that Jesus said, "Neither do I condemn thee, go and sin no more." I began to think that if God created the heaven and the earth and he made man also, then why should man have the right to judge me when Jesus openly forgives the woman and tells her to go and sin no more.

I began to think about my life and how I'd used drugs, stolen, lied, cheated and about everything else that I could do. Even after reading the chapter ironically, I still felt hesitant to read on. I thought to myself, I had done so much more than the woman in the story. I wondered if any of it and just how much applied to me. But I didn't stop reading there I continued to read the Bible from that day forward. As the days passed I began to feel better until one day I woke up and was standing in the mirror looking at myself and to my surprise for a brief moment I did not recognize myself. It almost starled me but as I took a second look, I put a smile on my face because for the first time in a long time I liked what I saw. I liked who I was.

I then thought back to the verse that I had read in the Bible which said that he would cleanse me, wash me and make me a new creature. Still after all that, I marveled. I couldn't understand how he could find me worthy and I still don't know why, but I am glad he did. I remember one particular question that was answered that day for me as I stood there in amazement peering at myself. As I began to say to myself, "I believe, I believe."

Those next few months went by pretty fast because in between praying and reading my Bible it kept my mind occupied. I was more than satisfied with what the Lord had done for me, and soon I began to notice that others treated me differently, not only the other inmates but also the guards.

Then one night I was lying in bed when I got an idea. I figured that perhaps I could start a prayer group amongst the inmates. The next morning I inquired about it through one of the guards, who was a Christian. She promised me that she would get back with me. It took about six weeks but then one day she gave me the news and it was good. I would be allowed to start a prayer group, but first I would have to fill out some paperwork.

I was so excited! We started the day after Labor Day. Only about eight people showed up but over about the next couple of months we grew to about fifty people.

A lot of good things came out of our meetings. Many lives were saved and it changed the atmosphere of the prison. It also gave me the opportunity to see what it felt like to achieve something. I also learned how to play the guitar which gave me a melody in my heart one that nobody can ever put out.

Then that infamous Wednesday came I vividly remember because it was a year since Vileen's accident. It had been a very hard year for me but that day was truly a test of everything I thought I had accomplished over the last year. All of a sudden I found myself and my emotions, on such a roller coaster ride.

But I'd made up my mind that I wasn't going to cry anymore and that I wasn't going to spend anymore time mourning. But I also knew that I had to make peace with Vileen and Mama. Once again I pulled out the old shoe box which contained those seven tiny books and I read them again. I began to think about the many disagreements Mama, Vileen and I had over the years. And I wondered why we never talked like we should have.

I guess it was like some twisted triangle where I spent my life in denial, while Vileen spent her's in search of something trying to feel the void and Mama she never stopped punishing herself until eventually she punished herself to death. Now all that remains is the many years that we wasted hurting each other as well as ourselves.

I wondered if there weren't some way I could make amends for all of the wrongs I'd done in my life; but then I knew that there wasn't. But I wanted to make sure that the future never mocked the pass. I must admit that reading Vileen's writings was one of the hardest things I ever had to do, but it tore down the wall, the one I could never seem to get over. It tore it down.

Finally the big day had arrived—the day of my release. I felt really good about leaving because I had accomplished so many wonderful things since I had been in prison. Now the first thing I wanted to do was to go and see my sister's grave and then work on getting my life together in hopes that I would someday be able to gain custody of Naomi.

As I walked down that long hollow hall, a thousand things flashed through my mind. When I heard the clank of those steel doors close behind me, I paused; but I refused to look back because I remembered the vow that I had made to myself. From that day forward, I was a new person. The old Ida had died in that jail cell and a new one was born. On my way out of the prison I gathered my things and waited for Sarah to pick me up.

She didn't have much to say and neither did I but on the way home I asked her if she could drive by that little white church, the one around the corner from the house. She paused for a moment but then she said "okay." I was glad that she did not ask me why because I knew that I would not have been able to explain.

But for some reason I just had to see it. Was it all that Vileen said it was? We turned a corner and I could see a tiny church in the distance. As we got closer my heart began to beat faster and faster and before I knew it, there it was. And you know something, she was right. It was as if it just drew you to it. I don't know how but it did.

As we got to the adjacent road Sarah stopped the car, but I beckoned her to go up the dirt road. Everything was so beautiful and peaceful. About that time the car stopped and I got out and walked up to the front steps. I saw the beautiful flowers there just as Vileen had said but the ultimate gratification was merely to come.

When I opened those doors to that church, it was as if the door to my life just opened up wide; as I stepped inside a feeling of such endearment came over me. Although I knew that I had accepted Christ as my personal Savior while I was in prison, somehow coming into the Lord's house made it all real to me and the way the sun lit up that room just amazed me.

I knew in that moment that something inside of me was coming alive for the first time. There was a picture that hung above the pulpit with Jesus inviting me—I knew that it was an open invitation not only into his house but also into his kingdom. As I stood there for a moment or two, I began to cry tears of joy because for the first time I really understood what it meant to not only fall down but I also understood what it meant to be caught by grace. With that I walked back out of the church and got into the car and went home.

When I got up the next morning I called the pastor of that church to let him know that I wanted to be baptized. That Sunday I got dressed for church. I was so excited because I hadn't been to church in a long time. When I got there, I sat and listened to the sermon like everyone else but I knew unlike everyone else that I was going to accept the invitation.

When the preacher opened the doors of the church for the invitation, I was the first one down to the altar. He asked me if I wanted to accept Jesus Christ as my personal Savior and I said, "yes." He then asked me, did I believe that Jesus died up on Calvary for me and I said, "yes" once again.

Later on that afternoon I was baptized and it was a wonderful experience—one which I know I will never forget. That day officially marked a new beginning for me. Here I am today it has been three and a half years now and I have managed to overcome tremendous obstacles. I have received an associate degree in business.

Through much perseverance I have also managed to gain custody of my niece Naomi and I am now working at the organization that my sister helped found. I must say that I am completely happy, although problems have arisen and will still arise. I have gained confidence in knowing that Jesus is my strength, and whatever obstacles lie ahead for Naomi and me I know that I am equipped to overcome them.

Then the mailman scratched his head in amazement as he asked, "Do you think in time you will be able to heal and move on?"

I already have, I replied. Because as I sit here on this porch watching Naomi ride her bike up and down the street I can't help but think about my sister, and my mother, and how much I love them both. In many ways they truly died so that I might have life.

It's a type of love that many will never understand because through Vileen's memoirs' I was able to see life through her eyes and in those writings I found myself. Once I did, it brought about a supernatural healing inside of me. Now when I think about Mama or Vileen, all I feel is an unconditional God kind of love, which I know that only God can give and I just enjoy basking in his tender mercies while he continues to heal all of my wounds.

CPSIA information can be obtained
at www.ICGtesting.com
Printed in the USA
BVHW042127290821
615475BV00008B/29